NO QUARTER AT DEVIL'S FORK

When Chilly Lloyd, a crazed outlaw, instigates a heinous crime, it seals the fate of seven other men. Now two friends, Brett Jackson and Reggie Satterfield, want to bring the killers to justice. Meanwhile, Stella Burdette agrees to run a chuck wagon for eight hunters — including Chilly Lloyd. But soon she must run for her life. And then Brett and Reggie fall into a deadly trap and are doomed to discover that there is *No Quarter At Devil's Fork*.

TERRELL L. BOWERS

NO QUARTER AT DEVIL'S FORK

Complete and Unabridged

LINFORD
Leicester

First published in Great Britain in 2011 by
Robert Hale Limited
London

First Linford Edition
published 2012
by arrangement with
Robert Hale Limited
London

British Library CIP Data

Bowers, Terrell L.
   No quarter at Devil's Fork. - -
   (Linford western library)
   1. Western stories.
   2. Large type books.
   I. Title II. Series
   813.6–dc23

   ISBN 978–1–4448–1236–7

Prologue

Texas, 1866

Brett Jackson decided to take the trail around Coyote Pass rather than the shorter route through the draw. The passage was not a major mountain pass, at least, not to a man who had lived much of his life in Colorado and Wyoming. However, the trail wound between several modest hills and looked like a good place for an ambush.

As it happened, instead of his route leading him away from a trap, it led him directly to one. Fortunately, it was not his own.

Brett pulled his mount to a stop as he topped the crest of a knoll, which allowed him to see the exit of the pass he had avoided. His gaze was drawn immediately to a dark form lying on the ground. After a moment, he perceived it

1

to be a dead horse. A rapid search of the terrain revealed what was happening.

Three Indians were moving about, as yet oblivious to his presence. They had captured a fourth man, a white man, who was stripped to the waist and spread-eagled on the side of a sandy slope. Evidently, the trio had attacked him from ambush, likely by killing his horse, and bound him to stakes at both his wrists and ankles. Watching them, he could see the warriors were gathering leaves and sticks, preparing to have some fun at their captive's expense.

Brett had a good horse. He could have ridden in shooting and maybe driven the three Indians off. But firing at a target from the back of a running horse is not the best way to shoot with accuracy. He decided to try a more prudent approach — as long as he got there in time to stop the Indians from starting their bonfire.

Removing his new Winchester from the boot, Brett edged his horse down through the taller brush, sticking close to what cover he could find. When he reached the perimeter of open ground, he was within a hundred yards of the trio. He dismounted and tied off his horse. Jacking a round into the chamber of his rifle, he started forward, staying low, moving slow and careful. He needed to get into position before being discovered by the warriors.

Time ran out for the stealthy approach, as the three braves had gathered what they needed. They began to pile the leaves and some of the sticks on the man's chest. One of them pinned the intended victim's legs so he couldn't buck enough to remove the kindling. He cussed them and called them all manner of names, but the Indian trio were unfazed at his outburst. They figured it would be only seconds before they sparked a fire to life. Then his useless oaths would turn into screams of agony.

Brett had seen a body or two after they had been tortured. It was not a sight he wanted to remember. This time, he could prevent the brutal torment and horrible death of a helpless captive. He took aim at the brave who had produced a piece of flint and allowed for shooting slightly uphill and the afternoon breeze. Cool as ice, he squeezed the trigger.

The shot stunned all three Indians — one because of the bullet passing through his chest; the other two cried out in surprise. Both spied the rifleman and went into action, grabbing for their weapons. Exposed in the open, there was no cover on the slope of the hill. Brett aligned his sights and fired a second time.

He scored another deadly hit.

The third brave decided their party had definitely lost its appeal. He abandoned the fight and darted toward a nearby arroyo, racing for his pony. Brett had the advantage and the range. He made a third good shot and the Indian stumbled to his hands and knees.

Levering another round into the chamber, Brett took a couple of steps to gain a better angle of fire . . .

The brave managed to crawl a few feet, then collapsed on his face and lay still.

Brett kept his rifle ready for instant use and surveyed the three downed Indians for any sign of life. There was no movement, so he took time to scan the nearby hills, in case the three had friends nearby.

Nothing.

It seemed safe enough, so he walked back and picked up his horse. Once mounted, he rode to the last Indian he'd shot and checked on him. By the time he made his way over to the slope, the fellow he had saved was straining against his bonds and lifted his head to look at him. Brett dismounted next to the spread-eagled man, but first prodded each of the dead warriors. There was no sign of life in their bodies.

'So how's your day going, friend?' Brett asked. 'Hope you don't mind my

5

joining in on the fun.'

'Wa'al that's just fine!' The man growled the words, but relief shone in his expression. 'Had to be a damn Yank who comes to save my hide.'

Brett grinned, taking note of the man's faded gray trousers and his Confederate jacket, lying a few feet away. Both of his wrists and ankles were tied to stakes driven into the ground. The sun had started to turn a portion of his skin pink, but he looked to be sound. Brett said, 'There's a rumor going around that the war ended last year.'

'You ain't seen any joy throughout Texas over that,' he snorted disdainfully. 'And you sure never heard any of us Texicans say we lost the war!'

Brett gave a more solemn shake of his head. 'You go on fighting if you want, Reb, but I'm done with the whole mess.' He paused. 'Of course, if you would rather wait until one of your Johnny Reb pals comes along, I can leave you here to fry in the sun.'

The man's tone became civil at once. 'Uh, now that I commence to think on it, I'd be one lowdown river rat if I was to hold a grudge against a Yankee who saved my life.'

Brett pulled his skinning knife from its sheath. 'Let it not be said that some of we Yankees don't know how to pay our debt for winning the war.'

Brett cut him loose. He noticed bloody rope burns on either wrist from the man's struggling and some swelling where he had been struck in the face. He didn't complain, sitting up to brush the dry leaves and twigs from his chest.

'I didn't even know those three were around,' he told Brett. 'I'm riding along and suddenly my horse folds under me. By the time I got loose from the stirrups, I was being set upon with a fair amount of savagery.' He shook his head, reaching over and picking up his rebel cap. 'I've been in more than my share of battles, but that's as close to dying as I've ever been.'

Brett said, 'I can think of better ways

7

to spend the day than having a fire built on my chest.'

The man got to his feet and quickly donned his uniform blouse. It had been torn off but was still wearable. He used the two remaining buttons to secure it and said, 'Lucky for me, those red devils didn't cut off my uniform trousers, else I would sure enough offend the womenfolk when next I entered a town or settlement.'

'Still dressed in Confederate gray, I imagine the occupation troops give you a little grief.'

'You mean the thousands of Yankee scum and black soldiers they use to police our population?' He displayed a sneer. 'Yeah, they ain't real fond of my type.' With a look of distaste at Brett's Yankee uniform, he asked, 'So what's your story? What brings you down to Texas?'

'I served under General Sheridan during the war. When Lee surrendered, Sheridan was sent down here as part of a contingent to contain Maximilian and Juarez below the border,' Brett explained. 'With Napoleon withdrawing his troops, I figure the job is done. Now, it's like you said, they want the troops to occupy the cities and ride herd on the local population.' He grunted his disgust. 'I've had my fill of fighting against other Americans so I resigned and mustered out.'

'I reckon them army jackasses up north are still put out because Texas never agreed to no formal surrender,' the man told Brett.

'Yeah, imagine them being narrow-minded about something so trivial.'

That caused the man to grin once more. 'I suppose there are some who might say we Texas folks tend to be on the stubborn side.'

Brett laughed. 'Too much pride can sometimes cause a lot of trouble. As for me, I'm on my way to putting the war behind me.'

'And how do you intend to do that?'

'I met a gent who is rounding up a big herd of cattle. The price of beef here in Texas is down to about four dollars a head. But drive those critters to Sedalia, up Missouri way, and they are paying thirty-five to forty dollars a head — even for those maverick long-horns.'

The news caused the fellow to scratch his unshaven jaw. 'I know a lot of the country above the Brazos River. That could be one hard drive.'

'The trail boss claims he'll pay top dollar to any man who sticks with him to Missouri. With all of the wild cattle running around, it should only take a month or two to gather a fair sized herd.'

'This here trail boss, he a Yank?'

'Never asked,' Brett replied. 'I do know he is hiring Mexicans, half-bloods, ex-Indian scouts and men who fought for either side of the war. He demands only one thing: the men must be willing to work.'

The rebel stuck out his hand. 'Reginald Satterfield is my handle — call me Reggie,' he introduced himself. 'Being in your debt, I'd like to ride along with you. I need to repay you for saving my hide. Besides, driving a bunch of mindless critters a thousand miles can't be any worse than dealing with Yanks.'

Brett took his hand in a firm shake. 'Brett Jackson, ex-Yankee, for two days,' he said. 'If you want to check up the draw, over where that last brave was headed, you can pick up a horse to replace the one these Indians killed. I'll pull the three dead bodies together while you transfer your saddle and gear. When you've finished, we'll throw some dirt over these bushwhackers, give them a farewell prayer and be on our way.'

'You going to pray over Indians?'

Brett patted a slight bulge on the right side of his chest. 'Picked myself up a pocketbook Bible, one published in Philadelphia, just before the war. Says somewhere in there that all men are brothers.'

'Yeah, wa'al these three brothers were going to roast my gizzard.'

Brett chuckled. 'I guess some family

ties aren't as strong as others. Don't worry, I'll give them the short version farewell.'

'All right, Yank. I reckon the 'Great Spirit' and the Man we pray to upstairs might be the very same.'

'You got another set of clothes? Those are pretty much worn out.'

'Having those red brothers tear the blouse off didn't do my wardrobe any good,' Reggie admitted. 'And this is all I have. I'm about as poor as a stray dog.'

'We'll stop by a general store in the next town and pick up some different clothes. These uniforms aren't cut out for rounding up beef, especially in some of the thorny brush around these parts.'

'You sound like you know something about cattle.'

'I grew up on a small ranch that my father still ramrods.'

'It's like I said, I ain't got any money, Yank. I'll have to make do.'

'If you don't mind being a little more in debt to a Yankee, I'll lend you the price of some clothes, boots and hat.' He gave a disgusted look at Reggie's head-gear. 'That Reb cap doesn't do much to protect you from the sun anyway.'

'Change my outfit and become a cow herder,' Reggie complained. 'Take up with a damn Yank and you're already changing my ways.'

'Go pick yourself a horse and let's put these warriors underground. We've got to join a cattle roundup.'

'Yeah, yeah, whatever you say, Yank.' But Reggie guffawed. 'I only hope tossing my lot in with you causes me less misery than being roasted alive!'

1

It was a warm Sunday morning, in the year 1871, at the Blackjack Saloon in the dirt-water town of Claymore Flats. Stella hated Sundays. The tables were covered with drink spills and all manner of grime, the spittoons had often been tipped over, and tobacco juice had been sprayed all around the nearby floor by the drunken revel from Saturday's crowd.

Pausing to stare at the smelly surroundings, Stella could not think of a single reason to enjoy life. Six-bits was her payment, a pittance of wages for cleaning tables, chairs, floors and windows seven mornings a week. The seventy-five cents barely put bread and beans on the table for her and Myron — probably the most worthless brother-in-law a woman ever had.

She wrinkled her nose as she began

to clean up a patch on the floor. It was a sickly brownish-yellow, with tiny bits of food in it. She held her breath against the stench, scouring it quickly with her wash rag and wringing out the puke into her rinse bucket. On a week day she usually changed the water twice. On Saturday or Sunday morning it was often four or five buckets for cleaning and double the usual amount for mopping.

Back to thinking of Myron, she couldn't really blame him for being a shiftless bum. He had no skills to go with his lack of ambition, a combination that made him worthless to an employer. The best job he'd ever had was a hostler at a livery stable, which ended when he fell asleep and let someone walk off with two of the stable's best horses. Most of his recent jobs consisted of using a wheelbarrow to remove horse leavings from the street or hauling trash to a local dump site for a business. He did as little as possible, concerned primarily with earning enough so he could buy himself a beer once a day and play cards in a penny-ante game at night.

Her husband, Rex, had possessed a little ambition and was the more handsome of the two, but his pleasant smile masked a volatile temper. At more than one job he had gotten into a fight and been fired. Plus, he too liked to gamble but seldom won. Even when he had worked at a decent job, there was never enough money. And when he came home drunk, broke and angry . . .

Stella attempted to shake the horrid memories from her head. Twice he had beaten her until she had actually lost consciousness. And he was not above using a belt to make his point. In spite of perspiring from the heat, a shudder ran through her. Rex had been a brutal man, while her father, a freighter by trade, had seldom been around during her youth. He was more like an occasional visitor than a father. Their mother was a sickly woman, who was seldom aware of anything going on in the house. Her older brother by two years delighted in mistreating her verbally and physically. Marrying Rex had been an escape from an unbearable existence . . . only to find she had made a dreadful mistake.

From her life of experience, Stella now looked upon most men as vicious and contemptible, insufferable bullies or abusive braggarts. They were dirty, corrupt, smelly and vile; they enjoyed drinking, chewing, spitting, and cussing and treated women with no more compassion than they would a dog. And while Myron didn't fit into that category, he was weak-willed, given to lying or cheating, and would never amount to anything more than a lazy, shiftless vagabond.

'Well, Stella, honey,' a familiar raspy voice broke into her reverie. 'I figured you might already be finished. Guess it was a busy night for us.'

Stella tightly gripped her cleaning rag, rose stiffly to her feet and faced the saloon owner, Mark Tygart. He was a roundish man, probably husky in his youth, but the muscle had long since transformed into belly fat. He wore an ill-fitting suit and a silly derby-style hat, under from which his shaggy hair dangled like black mop strands. He had shaved, except for his bushy moustache but he didn't bathe often enough to keep from giving off a pungent aroma. His thick lips parted in a smile, revealing brownish-yellow stains on his few remaining teeth.

'I've been thinking,' he began again, when Stella didn't offer to return his greeting, 'you could make ten times the money you earn cleaning up by serving drinks. This scrubbing on your hands and knees is no job for a fine looking woman like you.'

'I am not going to wait tables or sit with customers,' she told him flatly.

He moved up to where she was standing and, being four or five inches taller than Stella, looked down at her. 'If you were to bathe in scented water, brush your hair out and maybe add a little rouge to your lips . . . ' His eyes traversed from her face downward, lingering at her bosom and again at her hips. 'Put on a snug fitting dress that allows a man's mind to conjure up a mental image of you . . . '

Her lips pressed tightly with her ire. 'I'm not interested, Mr Tygart.'

The slovenly oaf reached out and placed a meaty paw on her shoulder. 'I should think you would enjoy having men treat you like a real lady.'

'Having some filthy drunken lout maul and manhandle me is not my idea of being treated like a lady.'

'There are other rewards for being . . . receptive to a man,' he said smugly. 'All you need is to have a little heart.'

She might have laughed at his attempt to cajole her with his impotent impression of a man, but his hand slid from her shoulder downward to rest just above her breast.

'There,' Tygart said, a silly grin pasted on his corpulent mug. 'I know you have a heart, I can feel it beating.'

Stella reacted swiftly. She squashed his leering face with her soggy cleaning rag!

Tygart immediately jerked back his hand and sputtered against having the filth and cleaning solvent shoved into his face and eyes. He attempted to back up, but Stella stuck both hands against his chest and pushed with all of her might.

Tygart was off balance and unable to see from the sting of the lye soap in the water. His hands flailed about wildly, trying to remove the liquid and grit from his mouth and eyes. Stella's wrath and forceful charge caused him to backpedal into a table. He hit it with such force he sat down on the tabletop and spilled over it backwards! He landed hard on his head and shoulders and lay there dazed.

Stella started to run for the door, but thought better of it and turned instead to the fallen man. Bending over him, she reached into his vest pocket. It was where he kept the money he paid her with each day. She pulled out the coins, then straightened up and kicked the man in the ribs as hard as she could.

'I won't be cleaning this pigsty again, Mr Tygart!' she shouted. 'I quit!'

While he sputtered and grunted from the sting of the cleaning solution in his face and being struck in the ribs, Stella bolted out the door.

She slowed at once on the street, not wanting to draw any attention to herself. She didn't really think the saloon owner would go crying to the law about an assault or the stealing of his money — which she discovered was a measly two dollars — but she knew she and Myron would have to leave town right away. She doubted he would mind as he hadn't found any decent work here and her job had paid barely enough to keep them from starving.

Tears stung her eyes, but she would not allow herself to cry. She was too strong for self pity and too intelligent to think God was picking on her for some reason. Even so, she couldn't help but feel depressed and helpless about her situation.

Damn, I hate men . . . and I hate my life!

★　★　★

Brett Jackson pulled rein as he stopped at the crest of the hill. He pointed to the small building down in the valley below.

'There you are, Reggie, Hannigan's Hideaway. Also known as the only tavern — trading post along the Cimarron River for fifty miles. I told you we'd make it here today.'

'Sun is already down, Yank,' Reggie countered smugly. 'It'll be nearly dark by the time we reach the house.'

'Gripe, gripe, gripe,' Brett shot back. 'And don't call me Yank in front of Hannigan. He never fought in the war, and being raised a Quaker he didn't approve of it.'

'I can guess whose side he would have chose to support in the war, what with the slavery issue.'

'I'm sure he blamed the Democrats who refused to free the slaves,' Brett said. 'Let's just not mention that either of us fought in the war or for which side. After all, Texas has rejoined the Union, so we're all on the same side again anyway.'

Reggie chuckled. 'That might be the truth, but I'll never be a Yank.'

Brett laughed and returned to the present. 'For a small fee, Hannigan's wife will likely whip up a hot meal, and we can probably sleep in the barn. I spent a night or two in the loft when I used to stop by.' He sighed. 'I'm sure looking forward to lying down on something besides the cold earth tonight.'

Reggie said, 'I agree. One more day of eating beans out of air-tights and freezing my hind quarters on the cold ground and I'll be as crazy as you.'

'I warned you it was a long way to my folk's ranch in Wyoming.'

'Yes, but you didn't tell me that it

was pert near as far away as our last trail drive to Abilene.'

'Durned if you aren't getting old, Reggie. You're starting to complain about everything.'

'Tell you what, Yank, if I'd have realized this ride would take us several weeks, I would have stayed back home in Texas.'

'And done what, punch cattle for another five years?'

Reggie pulled a face. 'Five more trail drives? Living like a pack of coyotes, suffering saddle sores, sun, wind, dust and rain? Being set upon by Indians, rustlers, and angry farmers or ranchers all along the way?' He harrumphed. 'No thanks.'

'Well, you didn't have to come along with me either. You're free to strike out on your own any time you want.'

'Not until I pay my debt,' Reggie said testily. 'Ain't no one ever claimed Reginald Satterfield ever owed anyone anything and didn't make it right.'

'It's been five years since I saved your

hide. You don't owe me anything.'

But Reggie remained adamant. 'Until I return the favor, I'll be sticking at your side.' Then he grunted. 'O'course I didn't figure it to take this long to get the job done. Maybe you ought to take a few more chances.'

Brett grinned. 'Things will look better when we reach the ranch. With my dad retiring, we'll pretty much run the place. The next trail drive we make will only be to the cattle pens outside of Cheyenne, maybe a hundred miles. You're going to be a ranch foreman and I'll be the ranch manager. Where are you going to get a better deal than that?'

'It means I'll be taking orders from a Yank.' He shook his head. 'I don't know if I can handle that. Might wish I had tried my hand at something more suitable to my personal taste.'

'Like tending bar? Or maybe you could take up a spade and hoe and farm your own piece of land? Better still, you could find a nice settlement and take on the job of town drunk.'

'I'll have you know, with my background and experience, I could have done something much more valuable for the community.' He grinned, 'I could have started up a Gentleman's Fellowship house and provided gambling and social entertainment for lonely men.'

'*Gentleman's fellowship* . . . fancy name for a whore house.'

'I commence to worry your chain is missing a link or two, Yank. In all of our time together, not once did you go along with me to a whor — ' he changed the title at once, 'that is, a *lady's parlor* for refined gentlemen. If I hadn't seen you lusting after every woman we ever came across, I might think you had no interest in the fair sex.'

'You're the type of guy who looks for a good time, while I'm looking for a woman I can respect.'

'Considering the shortage of women out this way, I'm sure to have more luck than you,' Reggie bragged. 'And that's what I'm talking about, a nice parlor and casino of my own, nothing but good whiskey, honest gambling tables, and fine ladies.'

'So all you need is money for the house, the girls, the roulette wheel, the oak bar, tables, booze — '

'Enough!' he said testily. 'If I didn't lack a few of the necessities for such a venture, I wouldn't be here with you.'

Brett took a second look at the trading post. 'Funny, as cool as it is, there ought to be smoke coming from the chimney. And Hannigan always has hot coffee on hand.'

'Does he have a pretty wife?' Reggie wanted to know. 'The only thing I've seen that's female over the last two weeks is my horse. Sally looked at me funny this morning, as if she was worried I was getting ideas about her!'

'Hannigan's wife is Indian, pretty much past her prime, but their daughter was ten or eleven when I went

27

off to war. Being seven years ago, she will be a young woman — possibly even married by this time.'

'Well, if the daughter isn't around, I'll have to fantasize about the mother, past her prime or not. Get to be my age and you become less selective.'

'I think that was Hannigan's motto too. He was on the short side of forty when he took the gal for his wife.'

'Sounds like a man after my own heart.'

'Yes, you and Hannigan call it selective, but most everyone else calls it being a dirty old man,' Brett teased.

At a dozen years Brett's senior, Reggie was living out the last year of being in his thirties. He still had a youthful way about him; his hair showed no gray and his only age lines were along his forehead and faint squint tracks at the corners of his eyes and mouth. Being relatively fit, he usually passed himself off as being about the same age as Brett. In an odd quirk concerning their friendship, Reggie almost always allowed Brett to make the decisions.

'So what, you don't think we dirty old men from Texas need love and female companionship too?' Reggie laughed. 'And there is no question, it wouldn't take much of a woman to be an improvement over my horse.'

'Careful,' Brett warned him, 'You'll be hurting Sally's feelings.'

They put their horses down the gentle slope, riding toward the trading post. It took another five minutes to reach the yard. A cow at the barn began to set up a ruckus when she spotted them. Twilight was past and it was nearly dark, yet there was no light shining from inside the store, no sign of life at all.

'Either no one has milked the cow this evening or she's in season,' Brett told Reggie.

'No horses in the corral, but the gate is open, and the place is dark.' Reggie shrugged. 'Maybe the owner left for some reason.'

They stopped at the front of the building. The door was half open and it was quiet except for the cow continuing to complain.

Brett dismounted and pulled his gun; something was definitely wrong. Reggie climbed down from Sally and held the reins to both animals.

'Hello the trading post!' Brett called, moving to stand next to the wall, careful not to be silhouetted in the doorway. 'Hannigan, it's Brett Jackson!' he called. 'You remember me, I used to come by every few weeks and stay the night. You in the store?'

There came the sound of someone or something moving around. Then a small voice whispered, *'Por favor* . . . please help!'

'Show yourself!' Brett told the owner of the child-like voice. 'We aren't here to do anyone harm.'

There came more noise, the scrape of something moving and hesitant steps. A young Mexican boy appeared in the doorway. His face was streaked with tears and he looked half-frightened to death.

'Who are you?' Brett asked, putting away his gun.

'Pablo,' the boy answered. 'I do thee chores for Meester Hannigan.'

'What's happened?'

The boy pivoted about to lead the way into the trading post. Brett paused to light a lamp, which hung just inside the door. Soon as the glow lit the room he could see gaping holes where the food and supplies used to be displayed. Notably missing also was most of the ammunition and liquor from the shelves behind the small counter. Following the youth, it only took a step or two before Brett smelled blood. Flies were buzzing about in their disgusting fashion, the way they always did around something or someone dead.

As the lamp illuminated the interior, Pablo grew sick and retched violently. Brett swallowed his own bile, forcing himself to not give in to the gruesome sight or pungent odor.

Hannigan lay on his back, his hands still clutched over his chest. The dark red stain was little more than a blotch on his shirtfront, revealing he hadn't bled much. The bullet wound must have been instantly fatal. His wife was a few feet away, lying face down. From the looks of it, she had been shot in the back at least three times.

'Miss Mary ez een thee bedroom,' the boy gasped, wiping his mouth from being sick. 'Meester Hannigan say to hide when thee hunters come. He worry they weel be trouble.'

'Guess he was right about that,' Brett said.

'I hear them' — the boy sobbed the words — 'they very bad to Miss Mary.'

Brett stepped over the two bodies and looked into the bedroom. His stomach began to roil and he clenched his teeth. Turning quickly, he retraced his path outside, not stopping until he was standing in the fresh air.

'I heard the boy telling you about it,' Reggie said reverently. 'The girl?'

'Dead. Her naked body is on the bed. I . . . ' Brett began, but was forced to pause and swallow his nausea. 'I saw her one hand; it looked as if she had broken her fingernails on her assailants. Probably scratched and clawed at them.'

Pablo had also come outside. 'I stay behind thee wood box,' he explained. 'Thee hunters laugh and talk bad to Meester Hannigan. One of them — I hear heem called Chilly — he ez one who catch up Miss Mary. There was shooting and more of them hurt Miss Mary.' The boy broke down again crying.

Brett patted him on the shoulder in a consoling gesture. 'How about you milk the cow, Pablo,' Brett softly coaxed the youth. 'It sounds as if she's really suffering.'

He sniffed back the tears. 'Si, ez much past usual time. I weel do it.'

Once the boy had gone to do the chores, Brett uttered a deep sigh of regret.

'We can wrap the bodies in blankets and put them in the tack shed for the night. If those hunters didn't take all of the food with them, we'll try and find something to eat.

'I have to admit, I've pretty much lost my appetite, Yank.'

'Me too, but we'll need the strength for digging those graves tomorrow.'

Reggie put his hand on Brett's shoulder, a sign of moral support. 'Maybe, once the kid is done milking the cow, he can tell us more about the men who did this.'

'Dirty lowdown vermin,' Brett said. 'Hannigan never hurt a soul in his entire life. Far as I know, he never turned away a hungry stranger, be it a weary traveler, beggar or wandering Indian.'

'I'd say we've a chore ahead of us, Yank.'

Brett gave his head a nod of agreement. 'Yep, it looks like the ranch is going to have to wait. No way we can walk away from something like this.

Those mad-dog killers are going to pay for their crime.' He pounded his fist against the door frame. 'They're going to pay with their lives!'

2

It was an unthinkable proposal, but Myron Burdette was desperate. Here was a chance to get a real stake. All of the work he and Stella had found over the past few months had been dead end, short term jobs. They lived like beggars, sleeping in a hay loft or a vacant shed, any place they could be out of the weather. Having barely enough to eat on what Stella or he could earn by working a few hours or days, it was a constant drain on him. He'd never signed on to be a husband, never wanted the chore of looking out for anyone but himself. This offer was enough to put them on their feet. And while it would be hard on Stella, it was the best opportunity they had come across since his brother's death.

All Myron had to do, him and his sister-in-law, was to provide chuck wagon service for a few months. That was it.

'It won't be that hard,' Lionel Kenton said. 'We got a late start and the guy we'd hired for our camp cook came down with cholera and died. You and you sister only have to cook and tend to the camp-fire chores so me and the others can do our hunting.' He gave a lusty wink. 'And who knows what could happen? After being with us a spell, your sister-in-law might decide to tie the knot with one of our party . . . maybe even one of my own boys. Now that wouldn't hurt, would it?' He showed his crooked teeth in a smile.

Myron had to smirk at the notion. He had no doubt she would be less than excited about this job, but they needed the work. To soothe his own conscience he did manage a shred of concern for her welfare.

'I wouldn't want anyone making trouble,' he cautioned. 'Stella ain't fond of having men buzzing around her. No one is to touch her or get out of line with her.'

Lionel raised both hands as if the idea was appalling. 'Hell, man, we ain't savages. Plus, when the boys and I need a little distraction, we'll ride into town and cut loose. It's like I was saying, we're just looking for someone to do the cooking chores. And your job would keep you right close to the lady all the time, gathering wood for the fires and water for the cooking and washing up. It will take the both of you to run a camp.'

Ordinarily, he would have not considered such an arrangement without first consulting Stella, but whiskey had a way of allowing a man to think more clearly . . . unencumbered by ethics and good sense. Besides which, Stella had nowhere else to go and neither of them had landed a decent paying job in months.

'You'd have to pay us a little in advance,' Myron said. 'Being out in the mountains or open prairie, I know I'll need some smoking material and my sister-in-law will need a few things too. It won't be much,' he hurried to add. 'I expect we could get by with a coupla dollars.'

'I'll give you ten dollars up front as a bonus for signing on with us,' Lionel offered.

'We'd still get the whole two hundred when the hunting is finished?'

Lionel displayed a candid honesty. 'Two hundred in cash for the two to three months of the hunt, just like I said.'

He hesitated again. Stella was going to think he had taken on another job where she had to do most of the work. If she did, then so be it.

He sometimes wondered what his brother ever saw in the woman. She could have been passable in looks, but sure didn't make any effort. She wore her hair pulled back, tight enough that it could have been a bundle of fencing wire, and he'd never seen her in a dress that was anything more than drab work clothes. She never smiled and only looked a man in the eye when she was cussing at him. She had been a burden to him since his brother had died from injuries received during a drunken brawl. With no kin and no place to go, he had been forced to let her tag along with him. But this job, maybe it was a way out. Stella had vowed to never take up with another man, yet she had spoken more than once about striking out on her own. He was saddled with her until he could pay to send her off to a big city somewhere. If they earned the big money promised on this job, there was a good chance he could get rid of Stella once and for good.

'Three months is the longest this will last?'

'Probably less. Snows come early in this part of the country and we aren't going to hunt during the dead of winter.' He let the words sink in and continued, 'As for the business end of things, we'll have money coming in after our first load of hides is shipped back east and credited to our account. Payment is a dollar and two-bits for every buffalo hide we take, plus there's a market for tongues and hind quarters too. Me or one of my boys will take the wagon to the rail-head whenever we get a full load. At the same time, we'll pick up the supplies we need and pay for it out of the money we're earning.' Lionel displayed a smug assurance. 'We all intend to make a fair amount of money on this little campaign. What do you say, have we a deal?'

Myron licked his lips, his heart hammering with anticipation. This was an offer he couldn't pass up. Sticking out his hand, he said, 'You've got a deal.'

★   ★   ★

The commander at Fort Bravo was a veteran of the war. He had been a general when the Confederate army surrendered, but peace time only allowed for so many high ranking officers. He had not been able to land such a position.

'Busted down to Colonel again,' Wainwright complained. 'Eighteen years, a dozen campaigns — three under Grant himself — and I'm given a commission here in the wilderness to oversee a thousand wandering pilgrims and a considerable number of hostile Indian tribes. I tell you, if I had it to do over, I'd have gone into banking or started up my own store back East.'

'I served under Sheridan's command,' Brett told him. 'Stayed with him when he was sent to Texas to patrol the Mexican border. I mustered out once Napoleon began to withdraw the French troops and Maximilian was pretty much beat.'

Colonel Wainwright smiled. 'I never met Sheridan, but I remember he fought more like a Confederate than a Yankee. He was also involved in the surrender at Appomattox wasn't he?'

'We blocked the possible retreat by Lee's forces after the battle at Sayler's

Creek,' Brett told him.

'A piece of glory for the history books,' Colonel Wainwright said. 'That's all any military commander can ask.'

'About these murders,' Brett got back to the reason for their visit. 'Is there anything you can do?'

'Do you know exactly how many men there were or the names of these loathsome butchers?'

'The Mexican boy saw them approach before the owner told him to hide. He thought maybe seven or eight. From the voices and names used, he remembered three: Chilly, Long Tooth and Max.'

'Not much to go on,' the Colonel said. 'Three first names . . . maybe all nicknames at that.'

Brett continued, 'The young boy said Hannigan called them buffalo hunters when they first entered the store. After killing the family, they ransacked the place, taking a lot of supplies and all of the large caliber ammunition. We trailed them for nearly a week but lost them when we reached a major road where there was too much travel to separate their tracks. From their direction, they looked to be headed up toward the Dakotas.'

Reggie added, 'Yank . . . uh, Brett here,' he corrected quickly, 'knew there was a fort out this way so we made a detour to see if we could get some help.'

'Buffalo hunters headed for the Dakotas.' The Colonel was thoughtful, but he displayed a helpless expression. 'That means those men will be hunting the northern herds, probably a few days' travel from here. Being ex-soldiers' — he raised an eyebrow and gazed at Reggie — 'for one side or the other during the war, I'm sure you realize I neither have the manpower nor the authority to send patrols up into that area. Plus, without full names or any idea as to what the killers look like, I don't know what I can do to help.'

'The help we will need is if we find them,' Brett said. 'Seven or eight buffalo hunters would be long odds for just me and Reggie here.'

'If you find them, you get word to me and I'll contact the nearest fort or send a squad from here to help with their capture.' He shrugged his bony shoulders. 'It's about the best I can do.'

'We're going to find them, Colonel, and they will damn well be held accountable,' Brett vowed. 'Three murders and a brutal rape have been committed.'

'There might be something else I can do,' Colonel Wainwright said. 'I know the US marshal. I'll telegraph his office and inform him of the crime and your need for assistance. I expect we should get some kind of reply within twenty-four hours. If you wish to put up for the night, we can house you in one of the barracks and you're welcome to take mess with the troops.'

'That's very generous of you, sir,' Brett replied to the offer.

Colonel Wainwright gravely shook his head. 'No, it's the least I can do. If it was up to me — and if I didn't have a wife and two kids still at home — I'd say to hell with standing orders and send a dozen men with you right now!'

Brett and Reggie were shown to a barracks by a friendly corporal. He explained that there were several patrols out, so many bunks were empty.

'You'll want to check the mattresses and bedding for bed bugs,' he warned. 'They aren't as bad here as at some of the other forts I've been in, but there are a few.'

'Like looking for apple seeds,' Brett said, referring to the size of the nasty little critters.

'That move like lightning and leave a bite that raises a bump and itches for days,' the corporal agreed.

'Knowed me a loose-moral gal once who used to keep some of those bedbugs for pets,' Reggie began one of his stories. 'Yes sir, she trained them to dance and come when called. Tell you true, when she said to pack your gear and git, you didn't hesitate.'

Brett groaned his patience. 'I'd wager

she never called her little pals when you were visiting.'

That put a smile on Reggie's face. 'Who would ever get tired of a pleasant fellow like me?'

'I seem to remember three Indian braves who weren't exactly charmed by your winning ways.'

'If they would have spoken English, I'd have had them eating out of my hand.'

'Appeared to me they were going to be eating off of your chest instead.'

'So how are you finding army life?' Reggie asked, abruptly turning his attention back to the soldier. 'Brett and I both had our fill of military life during the war.'

The corporal replied, 'I suppose we have the norm around here. Unless there is Indian trouble, we practice a strict regiment daily — tiresome drills and endless monotony, all wrapped up in a healthy bundle of repetition and boredom.'

'You didn't mention the dust and the

wind,' Brett pointed out.

That caused the corporal to grin. 'Yeah, the wind pretty much blows all the time.'

Reggie snorted. 'Hell, son, you ain't never seen a real wind. Why, down below the Brazos, I reckon back to a time the wind blew steady for seven full months, both day and night. Women tied their kids down with weights and cats, dogs and chickens all ended up blown into the next county. To walk you had to lean into the teeth of the wind and it pushed you from behind like a fast moving freight train. Wa'al, truth be told, it suddenly stopped one Sunday morning and everyone in town fell flat on the ground. Took the better part of a week for folks to learn to walk upright again.'

'I don't think all of the wind stayed down in Texas,' the corporal jeered meaningfully.

The three of them laughed and the corporal left them alone. Once he was gone, Brett turned to Reggie and said,

'Don't know how much good it will do for the colonel to contact the law, but I guess the horses can use the extra rest.'

'You know those hunters will be packing high-powered buffalo guns,' Reggie remarked. 'They carry a lot more weaponry than you and me.'

'If we can get in close, we'll have the edge with our Winchesters, because we don't have to reload after every shot,' Brett countered.

'Seven or eight men against the two of us?' Reggie said. 'The numbers will more than offset our two rapid-fire rifles.'

'You want to change your mind?'

'No,' Reggie was adamant. 'That would be *hell, no*! I'm just saying we're going to need a plan against such long odds.'

'General Sheridan didn't give a hang for odds and numbers. It was strike when they weren't expecting it, hit 'em hard and instill as much damage as possible. I reckon that's how we'll handle this situation, like we were fighting the war again.'

Reggie groaned. 'If you recall, Yank, I wasn't on the winning side of many battles. And I recall you telling me about a couple engagements you lost while under Sheridan.'

Brett stayed focused. 'We might have to cut them down a few at a time at the beginning. We can't guard prisoners and fight. If we capture them it will have to be the whole bunch at once.'

'With a hangman's noose waiting for them, I doubt they will be eager to surrender.'

Brett grit his teeth. 'Well, I figure we killed some good men during the war. Many of them were decent, law-abiding men. Just like you and me, their only crime was siding with their own state against either the Union or Confederacy. I'm not proud of having ended the lives of a few of those honorable men, but killing is a necessary evil that comes with war. What these hunters did, murdering a man and his wife, then to rape and kill their daughter?' He allowed the wrath to enter his voice.

'Those damn maggots have to be stopped before they can hurt anyone else. And I won't be one bit sorry to see each of them dying in a pool of their own blood.'

Reggie was a little surprised by the vehemence in Brett's voice. During their years working cattle together, he had found Brett to be the most temperate man he'd ever known. He was never without his Bible and was the most decent human being he knew. This savage offense was different and the Yank's rage ran deep. It was obvious he took the vicious crime committed at the Hannigan trading post personal. And while Reggie hadn't known the three victims, he felt the same fury as any principled man. Yep, those butchers better run hard, far and fast, cause him and Brett were coming!

* * *

Stella Burdette felt trapped in a nightmare. She was expected to live out of a wagon, camped in the middle of the wide open prairie, and prepare two or three meals a day seven days a week. Worse, her entire world evolved around serving a bunch of leering, dirty, reeking, buffalo hunters, all the while worrying an early snow storm might strand them fifty miles from the nearest town.

This job was supposed to pay well, but cooking for eight hearty eaters, along with Myron and herself too, was no easy task. Plus, she could barely tolerate any of the men. Lionel Kenton was pushing fifty years of age, and his sons, Max, Sawyer and Sonny were all in their twenties. Long Tooth Mason was maybe ten years older than Stella's own twenty-five. Skinny Taylor was near her own age, as were the two Lloyd brothers, Buffalo Rob and Chilly. Of the eight, the only one she could abide was Sawyer. He was more soft-spoken than the others and didn't join in on most of the rowdy games or vulgar behavior in her presence.

On the other end of the stick was Chilly Lloyd. He had the cool, passive eyes of a snake and she often felt him ogling her when she was working. He was the only man she had met who caused her to quake with trepidation from simply being in the vicinity.

The wagon was in a hollow this day, with a bitter cold wind blowing out of the north. Snugging her coat about her, she aimlessly stared at the chuck box. It was a maze of shelves and drawers of different sizes. There was a chest of sourdough starter, a sack of flour and all of the necessary utensils and plates. The coffee pot held three gallons and the brew was expected to be hot and ready twenty-four hours a day. The heavy pots and pans were stored in a hinged box below the wagon bed. For water, there was a barrel mounted on either side of the wagon. Other than the cooking materials, she had one change of clothes, a sleeping gown, her bedroll and an extra blanket. Myron chose to sleep under the wagon, as he preferred it over sharing one of the tents with the hunters.

The main cooking was done with a Dutch oven, a sizeable cast iron pot with legs and a rimmed lid. When in use, it stood over a bed of hot coals and then more coals were constantly piled on the lid. At the main camp-fire, there was erected a sturdy framework to support two hooks for hanging kettles or a large pot for heating soup or stews. Besides that, she had a dish pan for mixing bread and used a kettle for heating water for washing.

The meals consisted mostly of buffalo — using the fat or ghee harvested from the critters for frying or simmering — and cutting steaks, roasts or bits for stews. Sourdough was also a main staple and the men expected meat, hot bread, some kind of dried fruit and coffee for breakfast. The noon and evening feed included meat, potatoes — usually boiled or baked in the hot coals — beans, gravy and a light bread or biscuit. Most nights she would add dessert, stewed fruit, dried fruit pies or spice cake, made without eggs.

Myron gathered buffalo chips and wood, sometimes searching for miles around to get enough scraps of wood. The large herd of buffalo didn't leave a lot behind and often trampled the little remaining grass. As a result, Myron also had to find places for the team's horses to graze. He worried about that as he feared a couple wayward Indians might run off with the stock and leave the two wagons stranded.

Every few days Max or Lionel Kenton took the freight wagon and hauled the hides and buffalo meat to the railroad at Rimrock, where it was loaded on to a rail car and shipped back east. They would get a receipt which, once the shipment arrived and was verified, could be turned in at the bank for credit or cash. With ready funds since the first delivery, they would buy the needed supplies and return to camp. Meanwhile, the others continued to ride out daily, find a nearby herd, and kill dozens of the animals. They would skin the critters and stow the meat and hides safely for the next trip. Of course, there was one exception to the norm — when the men wanted a Saturday night in town. Then all of them would be gone for the better part of two days and Stella would catch up on her cleaning and get some much needed rest.

'There's a crude term for the kind of job I have,' Myron complained, having walked up without Stella being aware of his approach. She didn't jump, but rotated her head to see he had a gunnysack full of buffalo chips.

'Suits you,' she said sarcastically. 'I've heard the same crude term about what kind of worker you were.'

Myron set the sack down next to the fire, placed his hands on his hips and arched his back. 'Cold today,' he said, ignoring her barb. 'Hope you're fixing something hot and tasty for tonight.'

'Myron, I can only prepare what we have on hand. If you want pastries and a fancy dining menu, you've come to the wrong place.'

'Yeah, yeah, I know,' he whined. 'I'm just saying the guys will likely want something to warm their innards.'

'I've got beans, meat and spices in the pot for chili con carne, along with a few dried peppers and the last of our onions.'

'Lionel said he would be taking a load into town tomorrow and pick up more supplies. Better have a list ready for him.'

'For crying out loud, Myron!' Stella snapped. 'We've been out here for three weeks. Don't you think I know what I'm doing yet?'

Myron ducked his head, taking the scolding words like a little boy caught sneaking candy. 'I didn't mean nothing, Stella. I was only saying.'

'Bad enough you didn't talk to me first before you signed us up for this wonderful experience. No decent woman would come out here with this bunch of mangy, uncouth barbarians.

You've hired me out like your own private slave ever since I came to stay with you.'

'Hey, I'm here too,' he said with some spunk. 'What do you call that?'

'A small measure of justice,' she said flatly.

Myron looked out over the vista but the hunters were not in sight. When he spoke, his voice was guarded, as if he worried the sound might carry.

'These fellows are not the kind we want to cross,' he told her softly. 'I think they've done some pretty bad things.'

Stella might have ridiculed him for talking silly, but he was deadly serious. Plus, she could not deny the way she felt each time Chilly's turn came at the serving table. She put a steady look on Myron and asked, 'Why do you say that?'

He remained somber. 'I was greasing the wheels on the freight wagon yesterday, when a couple of them didn't know I was around. Max and Chilly were giving Sawyer a hard time about

something. I didn't get all of it, Sawyer got tired of the teasing and to them to go to hell.' He swallowed, as it took a real effort to keep talking. 'Max jeered Sawyer about how he had missed his chance. Then Chilly said, whatever they were talking about, it was as sweet as the best dream he'd ever had. That didn't set well with Sawyer. I took a peek in time to see him go after them both with blood in his eye. I figured there was going to be a fight, but Lionel stepped in and put an end to it. He laid into both Chilly and Max and told them to let Sawyer alone.'

'Do you have any idea what they meant?' Stella asked.

'No, I didn't catch it all, but it sounded like Chilly started some trouble at a trading post and the rest of them went along with it — except for Sawyer. You notice those two don't seem to like each other.'

'I did see Chilly give Sawyer a push the other day and cut ahead of him in the grub line. I didn't really think

anything about it.'

'There's no love lost there,' Myron said positively. 'On the opposite bank of the river, Lionel and the other two sons seem to be best pals with Chilly, as do all the others. I don't know what Chilly and the others did, but I'm for thinking it's something real bad.'

'I wouldn't put anything past the bunch of them. As for Chilly, he's the worst of the lot.'

'Well I wanted to warn you to watch out, Stella, so we don't get into any trouble with these guys.'

'It's too far for me to walk to the next ranch or town so I'll make nice and get along. Does that suit you?'

Myron hesitated. 'I know you had it rough with Rex. He one time bragged to me how he kept you in line with a belt.'

Stella felt the shame heat her face, but held her tongue.

'And,' Myron continued, 'I realize this job puts a lot more weight on your shoulders than mine. But it was the

only way to make enough money to give us a stake.'

Stella anchored her teeth and remained silent. Myron had continually pursued his daydreams, while they had been barely scraping by. The jobs she had to work at were the worst dirty chores imaginable, usually given to drunks or criminals working off a jail sentence. She had sweated over laundry, or done menial cleaning and scrubbing chores, to a low point of rinsing out and polishing spittoons. This cook wagon job was not nearly so bad as some of those, except for having to live out in the middle of nowhere and share the camp with nine barely civilized men.

'I've been doing some thinking about after we finish here,' Myron went on.

Stella regarded him with a hard gaze. If he'd come up with another scheme, some way of spending every dime they were going to earn . . .

'What have you been thinking?' she asked warily.

Myron suddenly looked sick, as if afraid to speak. She felt a sinking sensation, fearful he had thought up another wild notion as to how to spend their wages. 'Uh, well . . . ' he visibly swallowed hard. 'I thought you might want to take a little of the money we're going to earn and go to Cheyenne or Denver. You know, the way you've talked about a time or two, where you can find a place and be on your own.'

Stella's heart leapt with a guarded anticipation. She kept rein on the optimism. 'You said we would make two hundred dollars?'

Myron bobbed his head. 'About that, but I've got a couple debts to pay, and I'll need some start up money for myself.'

'Tell me what you have in mind,' Stella said, holding her breath.

'When this is over, I was thinking I could give you fifty dollars and pay for the train or stage fare to the city of your choosing.' He gulped again, as if he had to swallow his own eagerness. 'You did say you would only need enough to get by for two or three weeks, until you landed a job.' He appeared to hold his breath. 'W-what would you think of that idea?'

Stella showed Myron something he hadn't seen since she had joined up with him: she smiled. 'I would like that very much, Myron.'

'Really?' Relief flooded his face and he laughed. 'I was hoping — I mean, I know I haven't been any kind of provider for you.'

'I think it's a good plan, Myron,' she told him. 'I'm sure you won't miss me. You never asked to have a woman to watch over. However, Rex left behind only debts and not having a dime to my name, I had nowhere else to go.'

'All right. Then that's what we'll do,' Myron proclaimed, displaying a smile of both satisfaction and support.

A genuine lightness came forth to brighten Stella's usual gloomy mood. She had feared Myron would have thought up some plan to spend all of their money. With fifty dollars and a train ticket she could go to Denver, get a room of her own, find work, and begin to live her life as a free woman.

3

'There's hunters a'plenty in the hills and out on the plains,' the livery man said, pausing to spit a stream of tobacco into the dust. 'A good many come to Rimrock for supplies, and the railroad is handy for shipping too.'

'We've been to a half-dozen camps in the past two weeks,' Reggie told him, 'but we haven't found the men we're looking for.'

'And you've only got parts of their names?'

'A guy over at the saloon had drinks with Max Kenton and another named Long Tooth. He said they had a hunting camp up north. He told us one of their bunch comes into town every few days with a load of buffalo hides and meat to ship.' Brett wrinkled his brow. 'Mean anything to you?'

The old guy scratched his head. 'Like

I say, a good many of them hunter types come through here. But I recognize that Kenton name . . . though the fellow I'm thinking of, his first name ain't Max, it's Lionel.' He again paused to spit a dark glob of tobacco into the dirt. 'I remember him giving his name when he was over to the store getting a receipt for some supplies. I was there to pick up a couple plugs of chew while waiting for him to finish his business.'

'He could be related to Max,' Brett suggested.

'Come Saturday nights, we get a full house at the saloon — travelers and hunters, even a few soldiers. I did see that Lionel character last Saturday with two or three younger men — looked enough like him to have been his sons.'

'Sounds like we're in the right place,' Reggie said.

'Probably a day's ride from here, but where?'

'We could wait for the guy to show with his wagon of hides, Yank. Or maybe sit here and wait until they show for a Saturday night.'

Brett looked at the livery man. 'I've lost track — what day of the week is today?'

'Tuesday,' he answered. 'Plus, most of the hunting camps don't make it in but once or twice a month. You'd have better luck waiting for the freight wagon.'

'Who handles the receipts and transfer of pay vouchers for the hides and such?'

'Skip Balham, he owns the big mercantile on main street.'

Brett thanked the man and the two of them headed for the store. They found the store owner to be middle-aged, with his wife and two grown kids working for him. Balham was a sociable sort and told them what little he knew. Once they had stocked up on a few provisions, Brett and Reggie were back on the street.

Reggie asked Brett, 'Do you know this place, the one Balham mentioned — Devil's Fork?'

'I never heard of it,' Brett admitted. 'He said it was a fur piece up toward the northern range of mountains, but that isn't saying much. It's all mountains to the north and every batch of hunters names a wash, creek or ravine different than the last.'

'That's a big help.'

'We can also expect they won't be back for supplies for another few days,' Brett added. 'And they were in town this past Saturday night so I doubt they will come in again for another week or two.'

Reggie groaned. 'I think my idea about getting a room and enjoying a couple nights in a real bed just went up in smoke.'

'I hope when I get to your advanced age I'm not as much of a baby as you are.'

'Baby!' he feigned being hurt. 'Dad gum, Yank, I've lived in caves and survived on nothing but cactus and grubs for months on end. When there was game about I ran down rabbits on foot, sneaked up to nab a pine or sage hen before they could take flight and caught fish with my bare hands and ate them raw. I've gone for weeks at a time without sleep, crossed a hundred miles of desert barefoot and climbed most every mountain between the Canada and Mexico.'

'You were younger then,' Brett teased.

A smirk came on to Reggie's face. 'Like I said, I was sure looking forward to a bed and some clean blankets.'

'Time enough for that when this chore is finished.'

'You're saying we are going to head out now? Today?'

Brett pretended to sort his options. 'I suppose it's a little late for getting very far today . . . and we could do with a good meal.'

'Come on, Yank,' Reggie coaxed. 'Say the words I want to hear.'

'One day won't make much difference, not when we still have to visit every hunter's camp we see along the way. I'll get my spare shirt laundered, give the horses a rest and see about getting a meal and a room for tonight. That suit you?'

That put a wide smile on Reggie's face. 'Yeah, by jingo! That sounds just fine.'

★   ★   ★

Stella was cleaning up the dishes from the evening meal when she discovered Chilly Lloyd had been standing behind her. She gave him a cool, dispassionate stare.

'Did you want something, Mr Lloyd?'

From listening to the idle chatter and boisterous talk, Stella knew Chilly considered himself a lady's man. Better looking than the other hunters, he was the only one who ever shaved. He kept both his moustache and hair trimmed, didn't chew or smoke tobacco, and even washed before they went to town for their partying. His grooming probably put him one step ahead of most of the other hunters in the country, but Stella saw beyond his dress and manners. Chilly had venom for blood and a black hole where his heart should be.

The corners of his lips curled upwards to reveal his pearly whites in a lascivious grin. 'How about you call me Chilly?' he suggested.

'I prefer to keep my relationship with all of you strictly professional, Mr Lloyd.'

He gave her a once over gaze before replying. 'You wouldn't look so much like a spinster if you let your hair down once in a while.'

'The sun, wind and dust play havoc with my hair as it is,' she gave him a guarded reply.

Chilly continued to leer at her. 'My brother plays the mouth organ. If he was to give us a lively tune, you and I could dance there by the camp-fire.'

'I don't have the energy for dancing,' she told him. 'I'm often the last one to go to bed and the first one up.'

'Yes, you're a hard working little devil, I'll give you that.'

Stella tried to go around him to put away a pan, but he blocked her path. The action caused her to suck in her breath in alarm. She masked her apprehension and summoned forth her ready flash-fire temper.

'Get out of the way,' she said, loud enough that a couple of the others would hear. 'I don't have time for any silly games.'

'Maybe you'd like some of the games I know,' he taunted her. 'I doubt you've ever been around a real man.'

'A real man wouldn't have to make a pest of himself to get a woman's attention.'

The flicker of firelight reflected on his face, the dark shadows dancing like a host of evil spirits. Wicked was too kind of word for this man.

'Let the cook alone, Chilly,' Lionel Kenton spoke up, when the man still didn't move. 'Didn't you get enough exercise out there today?'

The tension was broken. Chilly laughed without mirth, his cruel eyes raking Stella like a firm backhand. 'Just looking for a little fun, Big Daddy,' he said, using the nickname he had given to the senior member of their hunting party. 'I thought our cook here might need a little diversion from working so hard all the time.'

Max uttered a crude guffaw as if Chilly had told a funny story.

'I'd say Mrs Burdette is a little too old for you, Chilly,' Sawyer piped up. 'I seem to remember you like them real young.'

Chilly's smile vanished. He put an icy look on Sawyer and a deadly sneer came to his face. 'You best keep your bean-and-tater trap closed, Killjoy.'

'Call me names if you've a mind to,' Sawyer shot back. 'At least I don't have to take my women by force.'

'I'm thinking you've never had yourself a woman at all, muttonhead.'

'Enough, you two!' Lionel commanded harshly. 'We have to get along together out here.'

'Come on, Chilly,' Rob called to his younger brother. 'Let's play some cards before we turn in.' He grinned, 'Long Tooth and Skinny think they can beat us at Red Dog.'

Chilly laughed derisively and walked toward his brother, who had spread out a blanket for a card game. He bragged, 'We'll spot them twenty points and still whip their pants off.'

Rob howled — his rather bizarre way of laughing — and gleefully began to shuffle a deck of cards. 'Yes, sir, you and me kid! We'll show them how the cow ate the cabbage!'

Stella released the breath of air she had been holding, suddenly feeling faint. To cover the rush of dizziness, she put the pan away and remained leaning against the back of the wagon for a few seconds.

'I warned you,' Myron whispered, having come over to stand next to her.

He pretended to be getting a drink, but the fear and concern shown brightly on his face. 'That man is loco-weed crazy.'

'You're not telling me anything I don't already know,' she replied back.

'Did you hear what Sawyer said, about Chilly taking a woman by force?'

'Myron, I was standing right here!' she snapped, keeping her own voice hushed. 'And I wouldn't put a foul deed of any kind beneath that disgusting man.'

'Five weeks,' he lamented. 'We've got at least that much longer with these men. The money sounded good, but I'm beginning to wish I'd never taken the job.'

'It's too late to do anything about it now,' Stella told him quietly. 'As long as they need a cook, Lionel and the others will keep Chilly in line.'

'I don't know, Stella. I wonder if we wouldn't be better to take my horse and ride off right after they leave for tomorrow's hunt. We would be almost to the railroad before they even knew we were gone.'

'And then what?' she asked. 'We have no money and our only horse is about on her last legs!'

'I guess it's a dumb idea.'

In a rare gesture of support, Stella placed her hand on his arm. 'We'll get by. It's the first time Chilly has tried to cozy up to me. Maybe he'll mind his manners from now on.'

Myron took the drink he had scooped from the water barrel and hung the dipper on its hook. 'I'll put the chips and kindling next to the fire for cooking up breakfast.'

'Looks as if you'll need to get us more water tomorrow. The other barrel is empty and the men will probably fill their canteens from this one before they leave in the morning.'

'I'll take the freight wagon to the creek first thing. There's plenty of room for me to haul the water barrels.'

Stella finished cleaning up and climbed the two wooden steps into the back of the wagon. She pulled the canvas into place for privacy, donned her sleeping gown and crawled into bed. She knew she would be unable to sleep until the men quieted down, but her real concern was Chilly Lloyd.

Being outwardly strong and resilient didn't mean Stella lacked the same inner fears of any other woman. Her father had been stern and dogmatic, while her mother's quick backhand was an answer to most of her own troubles. Her brother had tormented her for the fun of it, but there were limits to how far he would go. Her husband, Rex, had seemed gentle and caring when they met, but it had been a ruse. She had grown to hate living with him, but at least his weakness and violence was something she understood.

Chilly was different; he truly terrified her. When she looked into the deathly blackness of his eyes, she experienced a dread terror, as if she was staring at the Devil himself. And within the confines of her mind the words spoken by

Sawyer echoed again and again . . . *take a woman by force* . . .

★ ★ ★

'You think we got the straight of it from that gambler?' Reggie asked Brett, as the two of them rode out of the town of Rimrock. They had found a man who sat in on a card game with one of the hunters they were searching for. 'He might have mixed up who said what.'

Brett shook his head. 'I don't think so. He said the man was with the Kenton bunch — Skinny Taylor, he called him. And his pal was the one we've heard of, Long Tooth. So if the information is true, it would make it easier to locate the men we want. I'll bet they have the only camp in the country with a woman running the chuck wagon.'

'What about Devil's Fork though? No one has ever heard of it except for Balham listing it as their current location on the receipt he gave to the

78

man named Lionel Kenton.'

Brett gave it some thought. 'I've heard of a place some call the Devil's Tower, over near the Dakotas, a day's ride from Deadwood. But I'm guessing this name has nothing to do with that place. I think Kenton either made up the name or heard some teamster or hunter call it that. It could be a fork in the road along the stage route between Cheyenne to Deadwood, possibly somewhere along the Oregon Trail, I don't know.'

'So we continue our sweep north?'

'There's only the two large basins north of here. At this time of year the buffalo herds are scattered from here to Montana and that's only the northern herd. On the plus side, we know our prey is within a day's ride. That means thirty to fifty miles from here.'

Reggie rubbed his chin. 'The odds of us getting killed, should we find them jackals are pretty high, Yank. How-some-whatsoever,' he said before Brett could speak up, 'You saved my hide and I've never paid you back. I reckon, if you get us both killed, I won't owe you nothing for it.'

'You've an odd way of looking at a debt, Reb. I've told you a hundred times that the Good Book says we should help one another. There aren't supposed to be any strings attached.'

Reggie laughed. 'That there Book is talking about good deeds and charity. Any man worth his salt owns up to his responsibilities and always repays a debt.'

'Yes, but it isn't a debt,' Brett argued. 'You'd have done the very same thing for me had I been the one who was ambushed.'

The ex-rebel shrugged. 'Way I see it, Yank. I've been going nowhere since I first seen the light of day. If the price of my hide is to end the killing ways of a bunch of butchering mongrels, I reckon the trip will have been worth the ride.'

'You sometimes talk like a drunken poet, Reggie.'

'My ma didn't get nothing out of this world but pain. She was crippled by some kind of fever the year after I was born and died before I was eight. I worked to earn my keep from the time I could walk and did a better day's work than most men by the time I was twelve. I could shoot like Davy Crockett and trail game like Daniel Boone before I had all my teeth.'

'I would agree there's one thing you're better at than any man I ever met — you are the biggest liar and teller of tall tales.'

Reggie grinned. 'Another of my accomplishments, Yank.'

'Do you ever tell me the truth about yourself?'

'Every word is gospel,' he declared.

'Yeah, I figured.'

Reggie said, 'Truth be told, if I'd have had a father, he'd have probably sold me to the Indians.'

'Yes, I remember how taken the Indians were with you.'

Reggie laughed. 'Let's kick up some dust. We've got a lot of ground to cover.'

4

A light rain began to fall, but it was only the beginning of a much worse storm. The clouds rolling in were blacker than the smoke from a train engine pulling a steep hill — dusky, ominous and hugging the ground. From within the nebulous curtain there came the rumbling and earth-trembling thunder claps, while streaks of lightning slashed across the sky. It was late afternoon, but the gloom and fury of the tempest caused a darkness equal to well past sundown.

A gust of wind tangled the skirt between Stella's legs. Her plan had been to grill steaks for supper this day. That changed with the approaching storm. She hurriedly made a broth, then cut up meat for a stew and started it simmering. After a couple hours, she added onions, diced potatoes and seasoning into the big kettle. She was adding fuel to the fire when Myron waved to get her attention.

'The guys are coming in,' he called to her. He was a short way off putting the horses on a tether. 'Looks like they don't want to face the storm out in the open.'

Stella wore her only jacket and had a scarf over her head to keep off the drizzle. Using her hand to shield her eyes from the blowing rain, she counted all eight hunters returning early.

'Are you sure the horses won't spook from all of the thunder and lightning?'

'I've got them all hobbled,' he shouted back. 'They can't go far even if they break loose.'

She raised a hand to show she had heard and understood.

Lionel and the others arrived and worked quickly in the constant driving rain. Each man took time to secure and hobble his own horse. Then they carried their saddles and placed them inside the two fourman shelters. Lionel reappeared, after stowing his gear, and came over to the cook wagon.

'Good,' he said, 'I see you have something in the covered pot for supper.'

'Yes, I made stew,' she replied. 'I know some of the men were expecting steak.'

'This is a better arrangement,' he concurred. 'With this weather, we'll just be grabbing a pan of grub and getting under cover. How long before it's ready?'

'Probably another hour or so. I'm afraid I only have some sourdough rolls that I baked yesterday to go with it. Too much rain and wind for me to make anything today.'

He gave a nod of approval. 'I'll tell the boys.' After a pause to look at the approaching storm, 'You best keep to shelter and put everything you can in the wagon. I've seen the winds up here blow hard enough to knock a man off of his feet. We are using the saddles to pile against the inside edges of the tents to keep the shelters from blowing away.'

Even as he spoke of the wind, a gust whipped through the camp and rain pelted Stella in the face. She ducked and shouted over the noise of another roll of thunder. 'Holler when you want the stew and I'll get out the pans and rolls.'

Lionel nodded an affirmative reply and returned to his tent. Stella quickly began to stow away everything she could. Myron came over and fed a little more to the fire, then banked the coals and kicked some dirt and mud into a protective wall around the fire pit. When finished, he retreated to his bed beneath the wagon. There was a strip of canvas stretched between the wheels which faced into the teeth of the storm. Along the back, the steps blocked wind and rain from that direction, so his sleeping area was protected from most of the storm.

Within minutes the rain, wind, and lightning was upon them. The worst of it moved on after a short time, but it continued to rain. By the time Stella heard the call for supper, the ground was soggy and everything exposed was saturated.

Stella put two large rolls on each plate and the men used the ladle to fill their plates from the stew pot. She hadn't made anything special to drink, but she had refilled the three-gallon pot of coffee. Myron poured a cup for each man and the meal was taken care of quickly.

It was getting dark by the time the men finished eating, Stella collected the tin plates and cups. She rushed through the cleaning chores, working in a light, steady rain to get the job done, and then retired for the night.

Inside her wagon, Stella set aside her wet shoes and hung her jacket and clothing on a hook to dry. Donning her night dress, she crawled into her bed and sought to warm up. She heard the laughter of the men and knew they were drinking and playing cards. After a time, she could hear Myron snoring under the wagon. She envied the fact he could sleep through a buffalo stampede.

A short while later, things quieted down and the wind let up. The rain still pattered against the wagon, but it was more of a drizzle than a downpour. Stella was on the verge of dropping off to sleep when the canvas door was suddenly thrust aside.

'Thought you might be frightened by all the thunder and lightning,' a coldly familiar voice whispered. 'A woman ought to have a man around at such times.'

Stella rose to a sitting position in her bed, swallowed an instant fear, and stared at the shadowy figure. 'Thank you for your concern, but I'm doing fine, Mr Lloyd,' she said, inflicting as much calm as she could in the words. 'Besides, my brother-in-law is sleeping right beneath the wagon. If I need anything during the night, I'm sure he can take care of it for me.'

Chilly chortled, a cruel sort of

laughter, and sneered, 'That man ain't worth the wind to blow him away. What you need is the comfort of a real man, someone like me.'

'Please let me get back to sleep,' she said, battling a rush of panic.

But Chilly climbed the steps and entered the confined quarters. He sank down to his knees at the bottom end of her bedding, a mere black outline against the night sky. 'You don't want to make a lot of noise,' he warned in a icy tone of voice. 'Being a widow, you've got no virtue to protect, and you're smart enough to know what I'm here for.'

The whiskey on the man's breath hit her in the face like a gust of cold wind. He was drunk, and dangerous, but she was not going to be used like some cheap harlot. She reached for the nearest thing she could find and grasped the handle of a frying pan.

'What the hell?' Myron demanded, suddenly appearing behind Chilly, at the steps of the wagon. 'Stella? You all right?'

'Get lost, you bumbling old fool!' Chilly snarled over his shoulder at him.

'Chilly!' Myron exclaimed, recognizing his voice. 'What do you think you're doing?'

'I said to take a walk!'

'Come on, Chilly,' Myron said, showing more courage than Stella had ever given him credit for. 'Lionel promised no one would bother Stella.'

'Back away, you crazy old coot!' Chilly hissed the words. 'Or else I'm going to put a bullet in your gut!'

'You mean like you did to those others, the ones at that trading post?'

'Who told you about them?' Chilly wanted to know.

'You did, with all of your arguing with Sawyer. I don't care about that, but you can't be forcing your attentions on my sister-in-law.' Myron placed his foot on the first stair, ready to climb up into the wagon. 'Now, go back to bed and — '

Chilly whirled about and a gun exploded in the night.

Myron yelped in surprise and threw his hands in the air. He staggered backwards a step and sprawled on to his back in the mud.

Chilly held the smoking gun, his attention trained on the man he'd shot. Stella recovered from the shock of what he'd done and swung the heavy pan with both hands. The skillet smacked the vicious killer on the back of the head and the gun flew from his hand! He let out a howl of pain and tried to get his feet under him. He was too slow as she clouted him a second time, knocking him flat on the floor.

Men's voices called out, wondering about the gunshot. They were all stirring from their beds. As soon as they had their boots on, they would be coming.

Stella climbed over a dazed Chilly and hurried out to see how badly Myron was hurt. She felt the icy mud squish between her toes and a cold mist dampened her hair and shoulders. Myron's condition was evident from a single look. His eyes and mouth were both wide open and a dark blotch was on his chest. The life had already left his body.

Two or three seconds, maybe less, and the men would have their boots on and exit their tents to see what had happened. Chilly had killed Myron, an unarmed man who came to the defense of his sister-in-law. But she knew these men. They would never fault Chilly. They would protect him, the same as before, when they committed the murders Myron had spoken of. Their only recourse would be to kill her too.

There was no time to get her and Myron's horse — all of the animals were hobbled and tethered against the storm. Stella grabbed her shoes and jacket, which were near the entrance of the wagon, and raced out into the darkness. The rain was still falling and it was as black as the inside of a gun barrel. She stumbled and went down on her hands and knees. She shook the muck from her hands and staggered to her feet. Moving slower and more carefully, she began to pick her way over the uneven ground and around an occasional stand of sagebrush. Hearing the men's raised voices, she stopped, ducked down and looked back at the camp.

The hunters were cussing and shouting back and forth, moving around the cook wagon. They had discovered what had happened and there was some arguing going on. Being well out of their sight, the men were mostly shadows, outlined by the last embers of the cooking pit fire. Listening intently, Stella placed her jacket over a damp patch of grass. She then sat down on the garment, wiped her feet with the hem of her gown and put on her shoes. Stella picked out the individual men's voices as she worked.

'Damn it, Chilly!' Rob snarled at his brother. 'I told you to wait until the hunt was over.'

'It's done now,' Long Tooth complained. 'That there gal will shore 'nuff try and get the law down our necks.'

'We could say the shooting was self defense,' Max spoke up.

'Myron doesn't have a gun,' Sawyer nixed that idea. 'Chilly killed him in cold blood.'

'So what? We can shove a smoke-stick in the old sot's paw and call it a square shooting,' Rob endorsed Max's idea. 'I ain't gonna let no law dog haul my brother off to the gallows.'

'The woman will tell a different story,' Sawyer again took up for the truth. 'Ain't a judge in the country going to take our word over hers.'

'Hey, man!' Chilly whined. 'My head feels like a dropped watermelon. You sure she didn't crack my skull open?'

'You'll live,' Lionel said in a cold voice. 'Unless Mrs Burdette reaches Rimrock.' He gave a snort of contempt. 'Curse your lecherous hide, Chilly. You've put an early end to our hunt.'

'Not if we round up that gal before

93

she has a chance to talk,' Skinny voiced his opinion. 'She's afoot and it's forty miles or more to Rimrock. Ain't nothing else out this way but a few rabbits and magpies. Them hunters, who were ten miles to the west of us, packed up everything and headed for home last week.'

'I hate the idea of killing a woman,' Lionel said. 'I wonder if we could buy her silence.'

'Only one way to buy a woman's silence,' Rob complained, 'And we all know what that way is.'

'I still don't like it,' Lionel maintained.

'You didn't say nothing to stop what happened at the trading post, Pa,' Sawyer reminded him sarcastically. 'Killed the old man, his wife and daughter too. You didn't say a word against that!'

'You shut your mouth, little brother,' Sonny spoke for the first time. 'That was an Indian squaw and her runt.'

'The old man was no Indian and the

girl was half white!' Sawyer fired back. 'She didn't deserve that. None of them deserved — '

'Enough!' Lionel's booming voice ended the debate. 'We know what we have to do.' As was his habit, he had taken charge of the situation. 'Rob, you tend to Chilly and put him to bed. Skinny, you take the first watch over the horses. Wake me in two hours. I'll keep watch for a couple more and then wake Max. Come first light, we'll grab enough supplies for the day and go find the woman.'

Sonny pointed out, 'She knows to head due south for the railroad and Rimrock. She will probably follow the trail left by the freight wagon.'

'We'll divide into four search parties and find her quick enough.'

'I ain't riding with Sawyer,' Max said.

Sonny also did not trust their brother. 'Nor me either, Pa.'

'Sawyer will ride with me,' Lionel clarified. 'Long Tooth, you help Skinny pull Myron's body over to the ditch where we've been dumping our garbage. We'll throw some mud over him before we pull out in the morning. The rest of you, let's get to bed and try and get a little shut-eye.'

Stella rose up to a crouch and slipped on her jacket, which was still soaked from working in the rain. She knew from the set of the camp which direction was south, but the hunters assumed that was the direction she would go. Even if she walked all night, they would easily overtake her before she could reach Rimrock.

She was not very familiar with this part of the country, but she knew creeks and rivers were the life blood of Wyoming and Colorado. She had gone with Myron to get water so she knew where to find the stream. Stella shivered; the rain had increased from the drizzle and her night dress was already saturated. She would have to keep moving or she would freeze to death.

Stella moved warily until the camp

was out of sight, then she set off in a westerly direction. She would stick close to the creek and see where it led her. All she needed to find was a ranch or farm. Possibly another hunting camp, although the one she had occasionally heard the boom of guns from was no longer there. It made no difference; she had to find help . . . or she was going to die.

★　★　★

The stirring of the horse rousted Brett from a fitful sleep. He lay there listening to the light patter of rain against the poncho shelter, trying to pick up any unusual sounds. It took only a few seconds before he heard it . . . footsteps on the soggy earth!

Quietly and carefully, Brett eased out from under the blankets and slipped on his boots. With his gun in hand, he duck-walked out from under the shelter and used his night vision to search the area.

A shadow loomed up in the blackness that didn't belong — someone or something near the horses, a vague outline in the dark.

Quickly determining there was only one intruder, Brett crept forward with his gun ready. The person's back was to him. It appeared the man was disoriented or uncertain of his footing as the phantom staggered forward then backed up a step.

'If you're thinking about stealing one of our horses,' Brett said in a firm tone, 'I wouldn't.'

A gasp came from the intruder, but he didn't try to run or reach for a weapon. Instead, the person lifted both hands into the air.

'I . . . I wasn't going to . . . ' The voice was that of a woman! She took a step in his direction and fell to her hands and knees. 'I-I'm not . . . ' But she didn't manage to finish the sentence. She collapsed face down on the soggy ground.

'Boy Hanna!' Reggie exclaimed. He

had been awakened by Brett getting out of bed and followed him. 'What have you found, Yank?'

Brett hunkered down and lifted the upper torso of the woman up from the mud. Her clothing was soaked and her skin was ice cold to the touch.

'Ma'am?' He spoke to her and turned her enough to look into her face. She was unconscious.

'Get my clean shirt from my saddle-bags,' he told Reggie, rising up with the woman in his arms. 'This gal is nearly froze.'

'You found us a squaw out here, alone?'

'She's no Indian. I'll bet it's the woman from the hunter's camp, the one we heard about from the gambler.'

'You think?' Reggie asked. 'But how did she get here? And why?'

'We'll have to ask her when she is conscious.'

Reggie hurried to dig out the shirt, while Brett laid the woman down next to the bed and removed her saturated jacket and clothes. He used the towel with his shaving and washing kit to clean off what mud he could. Then he put the lady into his shirt and eased her under the blankets.

'What now?' Reggie wanted to know.

'The lady is nearly frozen stiff,' Brett informed him. 'I can only think of one way to warm her up so she doesn't die or maybe come down with pneumonia.' He explained what he had in mind and Reggie — after voicing sincere reservations — agreed it might work.

Brett hurried over to the creek and rinsed off the woman's things. Once back to the shelter, he removed his boots and edged carefully under the blankets. He didn't think he would get any sleep, but he would lay with his eyes closed and listen to the night sounds. It was highly unlikely anyone would be tracking the woman in the dark, not with the ground being little more than a mire from the rain. And they were in something of a cove, surrounded by a chaparral of buck brush and some wild currant that grew along the edge of the stream. It was a wonder the woman had found their camp. He decided she must have been following the creek, because they'd not had a fire due to the heavy rain.

Thinking back to what he and Reggie had learned from the gambler, there was little chance that there was another woman way out here; she had to be the cook from the hunters' camp. But what could explain her condition and showing up in the middle of the night?

Brett considered the woman might be related to one of the hunters. Perhaps she was a wife or sister. The gambler had said one of the hunters claimed they had a woman cook. That was all.

The woman stirred and a soft moan escaped her lips. He held his breath, fearful she would wake up and become hysterical. As groggy as she had been, and then fainting from cold and exhaustion, she might not even realize she had walked into someone's camp. She might . . .

But their mystery guest relaxed and her breathing became more even. She was asleep once more. Brett expelled a sigh of relief and closed his eyes. He still didn't expect to nod off, but there was nothing to be done until morning.

5

Stella's eyelids felt sealed shut and the broken dreams were like torn pieces of different photographs, flashing through her head yet making no sense. However, she was warm. More than warm, she was about as cozy as a lazy cat, snuggled on a soft rug, basking in the glow from a comfortable fireplace. The one thing puzzling her was the feeling of confinement. An unfathomable warmth oozed forth from either side of her, while a heavy blanket was draped over her and reached above her shoulders. She blinked and opened her eyes to discover a black canopy overhead. The first hint of daybreak greeted the outside world allowing her to see a faint outline of everything around her. She was stretched out in a bed, with blankets and coats piled on top of her.

There was nothing familiar about . . .

Stella sucked in her breath, pulled the top blanket to her chin, and sat up. 'What . . . ?' she stammered, looking wildly about. 'Who . . . ?'

To her utter humiliation and complete shock, there was a man bedded down on either side of her!

She mustered up a scream of alarm.

Before she could cry out, the gent on her right rolled out of bed as if someone had set fire to his britches. The second man turned to face her confusion and outrage. He threw up both hands in a defensive posture.

'Hold on, lady!' he said quickly, before she started swinging her fists at him. 'It's all right. No one is going to hurt you.'

Stella glanced back at the first man, as he grabbed his boots and hat and scrambled out of the shelter. In the single glimpse, she observed the tent was actually two ponchos spread between a couple of thick branches. She didn't recognize anything about her surroundings and pinned the second man with a hot, smoldering glare.

'You better start talking, bub!' she seethed the words. 'Or else I'm going to claw your eyes out!'

The man remained visibly calm, now sitting up, but his palms remained facing outward, either to ward off an attack or to soothe her fears and puzzlement.

'You stumbled into our camp last night,' he began talking rapidly. 'You were nearly frozen and passed out before you could tell us how you got here. We put our coats and blankets over you and then slept on either side, trying to thaw you out. Honest, ma'am, it was the only way we could think of to warm you up.'

Stella's eyes had adjusted to the dawn enough that she could make out the man. He was fully clothed — the one who'd run like a scalded dog had also been dressed — and this second one began to pull on his boots.

'You're safe with us, ma'am,' the man

assured her for the second time. 'I'm Brett Jackson and my partner is Reggie Satterfield.'

Stella might have introduced herself, but felt the sudden draft from Brett having swung around to get on his foot gear. She used one hand to check her attire and discovered she was wearing nothing more than a rather large shirt!

'I . . . ' she sought the words, but they lodged in her throat. She swallowed and tried a second time. 'Where are my clothes?'

'I rinsed the mud off of your jacket and sleeping gown last night, but we couldn't do anything about drying them until the rain stopped. Once Reggie gets a fire going we'll spread them over a line.'

Stella felt a new kind of heat and wondered why her blushing didn't put off a red glow. 'Then you . . . you . . . '

'It was full dark, ma'am,' Brett told her gently. 'I provided you with my spare shirt and — it's like I said — we put you between us so we could warm you up. I swear to you, neither of us took advantage of the situation.'

Stella suffered a renewed embarrassment. 'Of course you didn't,' she couldn't withhold the sarcasm, 'Men are so *honorable*.'

'Yes, ma'am,' Brett responded, speaking as if he didn't notice her cynical tone. 'I grew up with four sisters, three older and one a year younger. With my mother being a right proper lady, I learned to be respectful of women folk from the time I could walk.'

'The Yank is telling it straight,' the one he had called Reggie spoke up from outside the shelter. 'Sleeping next to him is as safe as sleeping next to your own mother. He's such a virtuous sort that, the last time he tried to do Confession, the Priest done ended up confessing his own sins to Brett!'

Stella ducked her head and sought to subdue her humiliation. With a great effort, she swallowed her pride. 'I-I don't have a high opinion of men,' she murmured. 'But I'll accept you both did what you thought was necessary to save my life.'

Brett put on his hat and left the shelter. Once outside, he told her, 'We'll have some hot coffee ready in a few minutes. Once you've had a chance to get your thoughts together, you can tell us how you ended up out here in your night clothes.'

Stella didn't reply, but listened to the two men moving about. They talked in hushed voices back and forth, and there came sounds of them starting a fire. She worried the Kenton bunch might see the smoke, but she had followed the stream and knew it went west for a considerable distance. From what she had overheard after her escape, the hunters were going to began their search to the south, toward Rimrock and the railroad tracks. She should be safe for a short time.

⋆ ⋆ ⋆

After riding for an hour and not yet finding any tracks, Sawyer opened the conversation with his father.

'I don't like the idea of doing harm to another woman, Pa.'

Lionel grunted his agreement. 'I know, Son, but there's nothing else we can do.'

'We should split up the money we've earned to this point and get out of the country. That Chilly is crazy and now he's dragged us into another murder.'

'No one is going to miss Myron Burdette. He was a wandering tramp.'

'What about the cook?' Sawyer wanted to know. 'You're going along with letting these men kill an innocent woman!'

'You saw the way she was,' Lionel tried to justify the chore ahead. 'She treated Myron like he was a dog. And she never had a good word to say to any of us. Myron told me the woman hated men and she seemed to hate her own life. We're doing her a favor.'

'Don't hand me that hogwash, Pa,'

Sawyer held his ground. 'You're talking to convince yourself that we should blindly follow after Chilly and clean up his mess. Well, nothing you can say is going to make any of this right.'

Lionel set his teeth, hissing his words. 'Chilly might have started the herd running, but we were all involved with killing those people at the trading post. We're in this stampede one way or the other.'

'You didn't shoot anyone and you didn't rape that girl, Pa. You and I haven't committed a crime. We should keep on riding and never look back.'

'Oh, just leave your brothers to fend for themselves so you and I can worry about our own necks!'

'Like you said, Max shot the Indian woman and Sonny was right behind Chilly when it came to mistreating that innocent girl.' Sawyer's eyes filled with tears. 'I still hear her, Pa,' he almost sobbed the words. 'I can't get her cries out of my head.'

Lionel appeared ready to bark a

harsh reply, to tell him to be a man or stand up for the sake of his brothers. Instead, he simmered and a look of reason came into his face.

'Son, I know you never wanted any part of this, and I do understand your feelings. But I'm as responsible as your brothers for what happened. I didn't try and stop them at the trading post. We didn't have the money to stock up on the supplies we needed for this hunt. It seemed that a robbery was the only way to earn us a stake. When Chilly went crazy wild, I was as shocked as you. Then the others followed along like they were part of a mob. I don't hold with what they did, but I didn't try and stop them. That makes me as guilty as anyone else.'

'Chilly went after Stella last night to rape her, Pa. He's like the son of Satan himself and needs to be put down like a rabid dog.'

'I can't risk having Sonny and Max being sent to prison, Son. Don't ask me to do that.'

'If we put the blame on Chilly — put a bullet in his brain and turn his body over to the law — that ought to clear the rest of us. He started the shooting at the trading post, he was the first one to attack that girl, and then, last night he went after Mrs Burdette and killed Myron. He's the one who caused all of the trouble.'

'I'm afraid shooting him wouldn't change much with the cook,' Lionel said sadly. 'Chilly admitted in front of that woman how we killed those people at the trading post. If she talks to the law, she'll blame us all.'

Sawyer's shoulders sagged with the weight of his argument. 'So we kill a woman whose only crime was taking a job as our cook. Damn, Pa, how can we be part of something like this?'

'Man sets his course for the best life he can, but it doesn't mean he won't run into obstacles along the way. We're trading the woman's life for the four of our own, along with another four men too. Eight lives for one is a fair exchange.'

'If you don't count Myron . . . and the three at the trading post.'

Lionel regarded Sawyer with a steady gaze. 'If you can't go through with this and want to ride off, I'll understand.

Sawyer hesitated only for a moment. 'I've nowhere else to go, Pa.'

'Then let's pick up the pace. If Stella walked all night, she might have gotten ten miles. With the rain continuing most of the night, she probably didn't leave any readable prints for the first three or four hours. Once we deal with her, we'll split the money and the four of us will strike out on our own. No more Chilly or any of the others.'

Sawyer didn't reply, but touched his horse with his heels and they moved ahead at a more rapid pace.

★　★　★

Brett took a plate and filled it with warm beans and a couple strips of bacon. He used his own cup for coffee and put in a little sugar, then took the meal to their make-shift shelter. The woman had set aside the coats. She remained covered with the blanket to her waist and had buttoned the shirt to her throat. She was sitting up so she could place the pan on her lap.

Brett handed the lady the plate and placed the coffee where she could reach it. He then sat cross-legged on the edge of the ground sheet. He didn't offer to speak until she had taken several bites.

'This camp you came from,' he began, 'would there be a man named Chilly and a couple others named Kenton and Long Tooth among them?'

She stopped chewing and gave him a sharp look. 'Why do you ask?'

'Before I answer that question, I'd like to know your story. How did you end up out in the rain, in the dead of night, wearing only a nightdress?'

The woman sighed resignedly and introduced herself as Florence Estelle Burdette — answering to the name, Stella. Then she took her time, taking bites between telling the story of how she and her brother-in-law had gone to work for a hunting party. She explained the events leading up to her arrival in the middle of the night.

'Chilly killed your brother-in-law in cold blood?'

A look of remorse crossed her face. 'It's the first time he ever stood up for me. I . . . ' she swallowed a rush of emotion. 'He was basically lazy, shiftless, and a coward, but he did try to make Chilly leave the cook wagon.'

'And this Chilly, you heard him admit he and the others had killed some people at a trading post?'

'Myron said Chilly and one of the Kenton boys, Sawyer, had argued about it one time when they didn't know anyone was listening. I believe Sawyer was the only one who didn't go along with the murders. I also was present when Sawyer taunted him about having to take a girl by force.'

The lady grew silent, her story told, so Brett relayed to her how he and

Reggie had arrived several hours after the hunters had left the trading post. He explained about the young Mexican boy who had hidden behind the wood box and been too frightened to come out, even after the hunters had gone. He informed her they had given him the cow to take home, so she wouldn't be left untended.

'Then you knew those people at the trading post.'

'I used to visit Hannigan's place before the war. I hadn't seen the girl since she was about ten or so.' His voice grew cold. 'We set out to find Chilly and the others and make them pay for their crime.'

'Just the two of you?' Stella voiced the question like it was a joke. 'You do know there are eight of them?'

'We spoke to the commander at Fort Bravo and he'll send a squad of troopers to help with the arrest. He also notified the law on our behalf.'

'If they find me, you won't have a chance to get help. You would do well to let me borrow a horse. I could try and reach Rimrock and, should the hunters arrive, you would be able to say someone stole your horse in the night and you never saw or spoke to me.'

'You said they expected you to try and reach the railroad or Rimrock,' he reminded her. 'What chance do you think you'd have?'

Stella firmed her stance. 'Myron died because he tried to help me. I don't want to be responsible for the death of anyone else.'

'The ground has soaked up most of the rain from last night,' Brett changed the subject. 'If you'd like to wash up, your clothes ought to be dry in an hour or so.'

'It isn't a good idea to keep a fire going. If those men see smoke, they might come to investigate.'

'We'll take our chances.'

'Don't be so headstrong and honor-bound,' she complained. 'Helping me is needlessly risking your lives.'

'Thank you for the consideration,

ma'am, but me and Reggie aren't the sort to turn anyone out, not man, woman, or child.'

'Arrogance and integrity won't change the odds against you.'

He took the empty plate and cup, rose up on to his haunches, and met her stubborn gaze with his usual calm. 'It isn't arrogance to do what's right, ma'am. It's the duty of all men of conscience.' That said, he left the tent.

Reggie had spent some time cleaning the lady's shoes. He also rounded up a towel, washing cloth and a thick piece of soap. He walked past Brett to the shelter, leaned down and dropped the bundle next to her.

'We'll avoid the creek for a spell,' he informed her. 'There's a nice spot just over the hill. Several rocks have formed a deep pool and the shore has a little grass for putting down a blanket to sit on.'

'Thank you,' Stella replied. 'It would be nice if I could rinse the dried mud out of my hair.'

Reggie returned to the fire and tested the material of the lady's garment. 'Another hour, less if she wears it damp,' he said to Brett.

Brett didn't say anything until their guest appeared from beneath the shelter. She had a blanket wrapped around her, held tightly in place with one hand. She carried the things Reggie had provided in the other hand. Without looking at them she made her way through the brush and disappeared over the slight incline.

'There goes a woman who has never known the love of a good man, Yank.'

Brett grunted his agreement. 'She's got an iron disposition a person could roller-skate on, that's a fact.'

'Seen me a gal one time,' Reggie began. 'She roller-skated on a stage down in El Paso. Durnest thing, she could spin about like one of them there ballerinas.' He showed a salacious grin. 'Showed off some real purty pink bloomers too.'

'I do believe you're one of the types

119

of men our lady guest has known in her life. It has caused her to think real poorly of the rest of us.'

Reggie laughed, but he remained grim. 'Let's cut through the fat and get to the bone, Yank. That lady has changed the situation and not for the better. Those men are all out searching for her and it won't be long before they come looking this-away.'

'Those are my thoughts too.'

'We need to get word to our pal, Colonel Wainwright.'

'That's a two day ride each way. Even if we were to get away safely those guys would likely leave the country before we could get back with help.'

'I've come up with a plan.'

Brett pulled a face. 'This ought to be good.'

'No, listen,' he said. Displaying a serious mien, he stepped closer and kept his voice down. 'I take Sally and head for Rimrock. It's only a day's ride. I can easily be there tonight and send a wire to Fort Bravo. The colonel can send a squad of men first thing in the morning. That means you only have to keep those jaspers busy today and tomorrow. I'll meet up with the soldier boys and be back the next day.'

'You expect me to take care of the lady and play a game of hide-and-seek for three days, without getting caught?'

'Wa'al, the plan naturally works better for you and her if you don't get caught.'

'You're too kind to me, Reggie.'

'Do you have a better idea?' he wanted to know. 'We could try and take them on alone, but I'm not real fond of going up against eight-to-two odds.'

'And what if you are caught by these guys?'

'Hey, I'm a lone rider, leaving from one of the hunting parties for a couple days in town. No one is going to pay attention to me.'

'That still leaves me tending to a mighty distrustful woman until you return.' Brett rubbed his hands together, turning over possibilities. 'And what if they get tired of chasing us and decide to get out of the country?'

'I know this puts a lot of responsibility on your shoulders, Yank,' Reggie said. 'You are going to have to keep away from the hunters while also keeping an eye on them. If they start to pack up, like they are making a run for parts unknown, you'll have to convince them against it.'

'How would I do that?'

'Steal their horses, shoot a couple of them, make them chase you . . . ' he grinned. 'You rode with Sherman, Yank; use your imagination.'

'Oh, sure, I can use hit and run tactics, with only one horse, while also preventing them from catching up with the woman at the same time.'

Reggie ignored the disdain and pretended Brett was agreeing with the idea. 'Glad you're in agreement. That makes everything splendiferous.'

Brett put his hands on his hips and glowered at him. 'Fool that I am, I thought we were friends.'

Reggie laughed. 'I admit you've got the harder job, but you have the patience of a desert wild flower. You know me and the ladies, I couldn't keep my hands to myself for three whole days. I barely made it through the night.' He feigned a shudder. 'Man, it makes me feel like I'm getting old. I can't believe I actually went to sleep while lying next to a half-dressed, modestly handsome woman.'

'You're right about one thing,' Brett allowed, 'I can't trust you to watch over the lady.'

'I'll get started right away. If those guys should pick up the gal's trail and arrive to see I've gone, the quail will be flushed and in the open. I don't care to be the target for a bunch of crazy hunters.' Another of his smirks, 'That's your job.'

Brett still wasn't fond of splitting up but could think of no better alternative. He helped Reggie gather his things and saddle his horse. Then he stood and looked at the best friend he'd ever had.

'You'll need to know where to find us, when you return with the cavalry to save our necks.' Brett turned and pointed. 'See the edge of that mountain range, the rocky butte where the ridges of those two major ravines come together?' At Reggie's nod, he said, 'We'll call that notch Devil's Fork.' He shrugged. 'As we never did locate the real one, that will have to do.'

Reggie took a moment to survey the area and get his bearings. 'All right, that will be our Devil's Fork.'

'I'll try and keep our friends from leaving the country and stay out of their grasp at the same time. By the time the three days are up, I'll be somewhere close enough to watch for you around that location. You bring the troops and head for it until I either signal or intercept you.'

'Devil's Fork, day after tomorrow,' he repeated. 'I'll be there.'

'Ride careful, Reb,' he told Reggie solemnly. 'Just like you did back in the war and there is a Yankee behind every bush.'

'You can trust me to get through,' Reggie replied. 'I still owe you my life. There's no way I'm going to meet my Maker while being in debt to a damn Yank.'

The two of them shook hands. Then Reggie collected his gear, mounted up and rode away. Brett was still watching him fade into the landscape when footsteps came up from behind him.

'Where is your friend going?'

He rotated around to face the woman. She still had the blanket wrapped about her, but also wore his spare shirt. Her hair was wet and draped down about her shoulders. They had no hairbrush and she had left in a rush and had no pins or clips to fashion or pull it back. Being clean and in the sunlight, Brett realized the woman was probably close to his own age and rather pleasing to look at. She paused at the fire and felt her clothing.

'I hope you don't mind if I keep your

shirt,' she said. 'My jacket is still quite saturated.'

'That's fine.' He smiled, attempting to lighten the mood. 'Besides, I never looked near as good as you in that shirt.'

Stella eyed him closely. It appeared she was trying to figure out if he was insinuating something vulgar or if he had tried to pay her a compliment. When she said nothing, Brett explained about Reggie leaving.

'Your friend is going to send a wire to the fort and get us some help?' she said, once he had finished. 'And they will arrive day-after-tomorrow?'

'That's the idea.'

The lady's brows drew together inquisitively over her rich brown eyes. 'Let me guess, you have some wild notion that you and I can keep Lionel and the others from finding us until your partner returns with help.'

'Shouldn't be too hard.'

She sighed. 'Not for a man who's duty is to right the wrongs of the world and bring evil doers to justice.'

'Don't you want Chilly to pay for killing your brother-in-law?'

Stella was about to say something back, but seemed to think better of it. Instead, she displayed a resignation to the plan. 'What do you want me to do?'

'We need to get together what we can carry and hide anything else.' At the curious lift of her brow he explained. 'If those men find the camp, we don't want them to know you arrived before Reggie left.'

'So they don't go after him,' she deduced.

He gave an affirmative nod, deciding Stella was a quick studier. 'We'll cross the creek and make for the hills. If they pick up our trail, we just keep moving long enough for Reggie to get back with help.'

'You might at least try and put some conviction in your voice,' she quipped.

'With luck, they won't find the camp too early today and it will give us a good head start.'

She sighed. 'I wish I hadn't gotten you and your friend involved. I've a feeling we'll both be dead and the hunters long gone before the army can get here.'

Brett groaned inwardly. Stella had voiced his own concern, but it would have been nice if she had showed an ounce of support. He had the feeling it was going to be a long three days.

6

Long Tooth Mason had learned a lot from the Indian scouts he worked with. When he and Skinny Taylor came on to Stella's faint tracks, he immediately knew she had taken to the stream and was following the waterway. Instead of trying to ride her down from behind, thereby having to battle the heavy foliage and winding terrain, he took to the open ground and started to circle to get ahead of her. They rode hard for a short way until they cut sign of a rider having been by recently. That caused them to stop for a look.

'Sonuva buck, Skinny!' Long Tooth growled, staring hard at the trail. 'That blasted woman shore 'nuff found some help.'

Skinny stared at the muddy tracks. 'You think?'

'This rider come from the river.

Can't tell if it's the woman or not, but the direction of the steed is for Rimrock. The wet ground makes it too hard to tell if there be only one rider or two, but we got to run him down.'

'Could be someone who happened by,' Skinny surmised. 'Maybe it don't have anything to do with the runaway cook.'

'Stella was commencing to stagger when we left her prints. She couldn't have gotten more'n another mile or two.' He snorted his confidence. 'Nope. She found someone to help or she stole a horse. This here rider is trouble.'

Skinny appeared undecided. 'If Stella sent someone and is still at the river, we only have to shut her up. Then it would make no difference if this horseman is going for help or not.'

'We can't take the chance,' Long Tooth said. 'We got to stop the rider. If it's the gal, our job is done. If it's some jasper riding for the law, we keep that wildcat cook trapped out here without the help she's expecting.'

'You're the ex-scout,' Skinny told him. 'Whatever you think is fine by me.'

'You remember that stretch of sand ahead? Ain't no cover for near a mile in any direction,' Long Tooth was thinking aloud. 'These tracks are fresh. We ain't but maybe ten minutes behind and the rider is saving his horse for the full trip to Rimrock. We can swing wide, ride full-out, and catch him out there where not even a lizard could hide.'

Skinny showed two missing teeth in a wide grin. 'Let's go have some fun!'

* * *

Brett hated to leave so much behind, but the horse would be packing double. Once they took to the hills, they would need every bit of strength the horse could muster. It was bad enough to burden his animal with two riders and the heavy roping saddle he had bought for working cattle.

'Would you prefer the front or the back?' he asked Stella.

'You're the man, the one in charge,' she stated simply. 'I'm sure you would prefer to be in front.'

He hesitated. 'You don't care much for men, I get that. But we have to get along. Both of our lives might depend on our working together.'

Stella gave him a steady look, appearing to lessen her stance without backing down. 'I know you're trying to help and I shouldn't . . . ' She gave a bob of her head instead of continuing with whatever it was she had been about to say. 'I'll ride back of you.'

Brett stepped up next to the horse. 'Here, let me help you up and then I'll mount when you're settled.'

He held the horse's reins while Stella managed to get her foot in the stirrup. She pulled herself up into the saddle, then scooted over the cantle and squirmed to find a comfortable position behind the bedroll.

Brett stepped into the stirrup and did an inside mount, swinging his right leg forward over the pommel and was aboard. He had already watered the horse, but they had only one canteen. Thanks to the rain, he hoped to find enough pooled water for the horse until help arrived.

'Reggie and I were on our way to my parents' ranch, about a hundred miles from here,' he opened the conversation, once they had crossed the stream. 'We were both in the war, but wound up on a cattle ranch, driving herds of cattle, from Texas to Missouri the first year, and then to Kansas for the last four years.'

'He calls you Yank, but you both fought for Texas?'

'No, I fought with the Union and ended up in Texas after the war ended. We met by chance and have ridden together ever since.'

'He appears to be quite a bit older than you.'

'Twelve years, but he claims five.' Brett chuckled. 'He's got more stories to tell than a small library. Lying about his age is one of the lesser tales.'

'He is older, but you seem to make the decisions.'

'Reggie ended up a man without a home . . . even a country for a time. He let me point the direction and we went. It's a solid friendship where we both depend on and trust the other.'

'Sounds like you two should be married,' she jibed.

Brett ignored the cynicism. 'I prefer someone a bit more feminine,' he said. 'And a marriage needs both partners to be willing to share different responsibilities and do for the other. We mostly do for ourselves.'

'I've not seen a marriage like that,' she said quietly.

'You need to meet my mom and dad. My father dotes on Mom like she was the most special thing in his life, while my mother does everything in the world she can to please my dad. That's what I mean about doing for someone else.'

'I didn't see much of my father and my mother only spoke to yell or criticize me. My older brother was

Mom's favorite child and he loved to torment me — both verbally and physically. Then my husband was a two-faced brute, who pretended to be sweet and gentle in public, but was a drunkard who enjoyed slapping me around in private. When he died suddenly, my only option was to become a personal slave for Myron. He was a lazy drifter who dreamed of making big money without having to work for it. We barely got by on what little I could earn at the jobs he found for me.' She uttered a caustic laugh. 'He seldom found work for himself.'

'You did say he tried to help you last night?'

Stella sighed. 'Yes, weak and spineless as he was, he did try to stop Chilly. I . . . I didn't know he had that much courage.'

Brett reached the summit of a small hill and took a moment to search the open country. There was nothing in sight.

'Your camp is which way,' he pointed, 'over that way?'

'Yes, I would guess maybe five or six miles.'

'Then we'll keep going in this direction. If we can get close enough for a look, we might discover what those guys have in mind.'

'Maybe we could slip down to the wagon and get my clothes and personal things,' she said hopefully.

'I wouldn't count on it. We can't let them spot us or find any readable prints. We have to keep hidden as long as we can.'

'I understand.'

Brett said, 'I'm sorry that I don't have another change of clothes. We burned the work clothes before we left Texas and I only have the one extra shirt.'

'Yes,' her voice was terse, 'I said I understand.'

Brett grit his teeth, nudged Trixie into a walk and thought, *Yep, Brett, old buddy, three days is likely to seem*

136

longer than that last five-hundred mile cattle drive!

* * *

Reggie felt a sharp sting down his left leg as Sally suddenly buckled to her knees. Even as the horse fell on her side, Reggie heard the distant report of a big gun. His automatic reflexes were all that prevented his right leg from being pinned under Sally. The trusty horse thrashed out with her hoofs for a moment and then lay still.

Ducking behind her for cover, Reggie knew the shooter was well up into the hills and out of pistol range. The problem was, Sally was lying on his rifle so he couldn't get to the weapon without exposing himself to fire.

Dust kicked up a few feet from him and he realized another shot had come from the front. That meant there were at least two ambushers and both had high powered guns. He scrambled over Sally and wedged himself in next to her belly. Her hind legs now offered added protection from the two shooters. He held his breath wondering if he would be killed with a shot from a third shooter, but it was totally silent.

Reggie considered the situation: at least two riflemen, one off to his left and one in front of him. They were both a fair distance off, but they had chosen the location of their ambush well. There wasn't so much as a blade of grass within a hundred yards going any direction. The sun would be up for several more hours, but darkness would not aid him in an escape. The moon would be nearly full and there wasn't a cloud to be seen in the sky. Trapped against a background of white sand and caked earth he would be spotted before he moved ten feet in daylight or after dark.

In no imminent danger at the moment, he quickly checked his leg. The bullet had only nicked the skin enough to make it bleed, so he had been lucky to this point. He took a moment and used his bandanna as a bandage. Then he checked the loads in his pistol and kept watch for a time. Finally, he spied a rider from the hills off to his left. The man took a casual ride around toward the second man to his front. The other got aboard his horse and rode to meet him.

Gotta be damn Yanks! he thought sourly. Somehow the hunters had figured out the plan and managed to get ahead of him. With his horse dead, they knew they had their prey trapped. The dirty bushwhackers were showing their confidence, riding out in the open, knowing they were well out of range. The smug weasels were having a casual confab to decide his fate.

Reggie took a frantic look around. If he took off running, it was maybe a half mile to the nearest gully. He gave up the idea at once. Even if he stayed low to the ground and the wound in his leg didn't bother him, he would be exposed to their fire for a full two or three minutes. For practiced men — and these men were shooting buffalo every day — with either a Sharps .50 caliber or maybe a Remington Rolling-Block single-shot .44-90, he would still need them to miss about three or four shots each. Considering the man who shot first had taken down Sally and the other had only missed by inches, he couldn't trust to luck to outrun their shooting.

Reggie watched the two men. They were talking back and forth, all the while keeping alert in case Reggie dared to show himself. There was no hurry on their part; Reggie wasn't going anywhere . . . and that was also troublesome. He couldn't very well send for help while waiting to be killed.

But what to do?

After an hour and a careful assessment of the situation, Reggie understood their plan. They were waiting for dark so they could move into position for a kill shot at daylight. Because he had the horse to hide behind, the only way to get at him was from the rear. The terrain to the back of him, however, was a casual slope that elevated several feet higher than where he was before it gradually leveled off. For a man to come from that side, he would have to circle around and work his way far enough down the slope to get a clear shot at the target. That meant moving to within normal rifle range or closer. With one of them to pin him down, the other could maneuver around and find a good kill shot. He would be easy meat for the two hunters.

Lying there behind his favorite horse, Reggie considered his past. Most men facing death would like to look back and think he had made a difference. Reggie had lived only for himself up until the war. When Texas asked for volunteers, it had been a whim, a new taste of excitement for him. He didn't know the whys of the conflict — didn't care one way or the other. It only meant he would belong and that was a feeling he hadn't felt since he was a little kid. Passed around to one family or the next, he worked like a stray dog for a meal and shelter for a few nights at a time. He had not belonged to anyone or anything.

Once he put on the uniform, he felt a part of something, but there was little satisfaction fighting a war. It was not a good life, living in a tent, sharing your life with a thousand different strangers, then watching the few who meant something to you ending up wounded, sick, or killed. Reggie had gradually become a loner, even in the Confederate army. When he returned to Texas there was no work, no money, and times were bitter and hard for everyone. He tried to keep the war alive, wanting to feel he still belonged to what little the army had offered, but it only brought him trouble.

Riding into an Indian trap could have been the end of a lonely, unhappy, wasted life. But everything changed when Brett Jackson arrived on the scene. He not only saved him from death, he saved him from the life he'd been living. He accepted Reggie like a friend, without reservations, although he often scolded him for his drinking or gambling like a watchful big brother.

During the roundups and cattle drives Reggie had learned what true friendship was all about. The two of them froze together in winter and roasted and strangled on dust in the heat of summer. They worked hard, had fun when they could, and would hunt and fish together when they got the chance. During a blizzard or hole up in a cabin for days on end, Brett would be there, playing games, talking about his home, or reading from the Bible he always carried. Being his pal was being his brother and it was the attachment he had never known during his life; it was a chance to simply belong.

He stared out at the two riders. They were smug, cocky even, knowing Reggie was pinned down and had nowhere to run. He would be an easy kill . . . or so they thought. But Reggie had a burning desire to survive, because his friend needed him. Brett was counting on him to get help or be there to help himself.

Death was not an option while his best friend's life was at stake. He had to figure a way to turn the tables.

As darkness began to cover the land, Reggie watched the two distant shadows. One rode off, but the other remained poised where he could watch Reggie for the night. They knew he couldn't go anywhere, and sometime, before the first rays of light, those two would move. When daylight came, they would be in position to kill him.

Reggie glared at the sentry, his eyes burning from the sun and wind. 'You think you've got this Johnny Reb trussed up like a calf for branding.' He snorted his contempt. 'Wa'al, think again, you blue-bellied bushwhackers.'

Once he was hidden by the shadows of night, he patted his fallen horse. 'You were a good, loyal horse, Sally, my girl,' he said solemnly. 'I just need one more favor and I'll let you rest.'

*　*　*

Lionel and the others met back at camp. Skinny arrived an hour after dark and told them about the man they had pinned down.

'So the girl followed the river,' Chilly remarked, after hearing the story. 'No wonder we couldn't find her tracks. We'll go have a look in the morning.'

'What about you?' Max asked Skinny. 'You think the guy will stick it out all night?'

'Against that white background, he could slither like a snake and Long Tooth would still blow a dozen holes in him. From where he's sitting, Long Tooth can see the whole basin. Once I get back, we'll each catch a little shut-eye. Come daybreak, we'll be around in back of him. Won't be no trouble to put an end to whoever the guy is.'

'So we kill another innocent man,' Sawyer said dejectedly. 'Chilly, I hope to hell I'm there to watch when they string you up.' He paused to spit into the dirt. 'Even if I'm next in line, I pray

I get to watch you die first!'

'That's enough!' Lionel scolded his son. 'We have to do whatever it takes to get out of this mess. Then we'll gather what hides we have and make for Rimrock. Once we get our money in hand, we'll split it up and go our separate ways.'

Chilly glared at Sawyer. 'Yeah, you best make sure you go a different direction than me . . . else I'm liable to wind up killing you, boy.'

'I wouldn't be as easy as Myron or a woman!'

Lionel moved between Chilly and his son. 'I said *enough*!' he bellowed at the two of them. 'Until this chore is finished we can't be fighting amongst ourselves.'

'I'll be heading back,' Skinny told the group. 'You boys find that gal tomorrow and we're in the clear.'

Sawyer turned for their tent. 'Yeah, in the clear,' he repeated in a mocking voice. 'Be a damn shame if we didn't kill a half-dozen more people before we part company . . . all because of Chilly.'

'You best grow a backbone, little brother!' Sonny scolded him. 'Max and me will do our part. You need to buck up and join the family.'

Sawyer paused at the entrance to their shelter.

'Don't worry about me, Sonny. I'll be right by your side when they put the noose around all of our necks.'

Lionel didn't allow for any more name calling or threats. As was his habit, he took charge. 'We need to keep someone close by the camp, in case that woman tries to circle back and grab one of the team horses.'

'What if she found a camp of several men to help her?' Rob asked.

'They only sent one man to Rimrock,' Lionel surmised. 'If there were a bunch of them, they would have escorted her to town or even tried to come after us themselves. No, I'd say she found a small camp — two or three men maybe.'

'We'll know what we're up against

when we find where she ran into them,'
Max said.

Lionel ordered, 'We'll do like last
night. Everyone pulls an hour on guard
duty. I'll take the first watch.'

'Don't bother waking Sawyer, Big
Daddy,' Chilly warned. 'I wager he'd
allow the cook to grab a horse and ride
off without saying a word.'

'Probably saddle it for her,' Max
agreed.

Lionel ignored the chatter. 'All right,
everyone will pull a shift but Sawyer.'

★   ★   ★

Shortly after sunset, Brett found a
sheltered cove between some sizeable
boulders. It took some searching to find
enough smokeless wood, bark and dried
leaves to make a carefully tended fire.
He used the only pan he had packed for
frying up their meager supper while
Stella busied herself making a lean-to
out of the single poncho. As there was
no extra bedding, she used the

saddle-blanket as a ground sheet and made up a single bed. Being warmer this night, she folded her jacket for a pillow for herself and did the same for Brett with his coat.

Beans again, with a couple strips of salt pork, a hard roll and water. It was not a feast, but it would have to hold them until the following night. For breakfast, they would have only a roll and a piece or two of jerky.

After a quiet meal, Brett rubbed down his horse and staked her on a lead rope so she could forage for what leaves or grass she could find. He returned to discover Stella holding the material of her sleeping gown to one side so she could feel and peer at the insides of her legs. She immediately pulled the cloth back to cover herself at his approach.

'Didn't think about that,' Brett said, experiencing an instant compassion. 'I'll bet you were rubbed raw riding on the back of the horse all day.'

'I've never done much riding,' she

admitted. 'And the saddle-blanket is quite rough.'

Brett grabbed up one of the clean tin plates. 'I'll be back in a few minutes. I spotted a patch of aloe just before we stopped for the night.'

'Aloe?'

He ignored her curiosity and hurried to find the plant. It was near where he had picketed the horse so he found it without too much searching. The plant resembled cactus, but the thorn-like nubs were not as sharp. Taking hold of one of the pointed inner stalks, he took his knife and cut through the stem. He held the leaf firmly and cut into it. He was careful not to allow the yellow-green sap to collect on to the plate, only the transparent fluid. It only bled a few drops so he crushed the pulp and was able to collect a little more. He repeated this with other stalks until he had about two spoons of liquid. Then he returned to camp.

'This is something of an Indian remedy,' he explained to Stella. 'Apply this like you would an ointment and it will help to soothe away some of the tenderness.'

'What is it?'

'It's called aloe vera. An old timer showed Reggie and me the trick when we were on a cattle drive.'

He set the pan down next to the bed and put his back to her. 'I'll cover the fire while you apply the lotion.'

Actually, there was little to do about the fire. He kicked a little dirt over the dead coals and kept his back to the woman. After a couple minutes, she spoke up.

'That does feel a little better.'

Brett pivoted around and saw the lady was under the blankets. He retrieved the pan, wiped it clean and put it away. Then he hesitated, uncertain as to what came next.

'You're not going to stand guard all night?' she asked. 'That would be a total waste of time. I doubt those men are going to be searching out in the hills after dark.'

'I reckon you're right about that, ma'am.'

'So come to bed.'

Brett felt uncomfortable at hearing those words from a woman, but he did as she instructed. He removed his gun, hat and boots and eased in alongside of Stella. Then he carefully draped the blanket over his body and adjusted his folded coat to make it more comfortable to lay his head against.

'You didn't ask me one question today,' Stella said softly.

'I didn't wish to intrude on your thoughts,' he replied. 'You lost your brother-in-law yesterday and are facing the world all on your own. I figured you would be doing a fair share of contemplating.'

'No more than you,' she returned. 'After all, you're the one who got stuck with me.'

'Actually, you made my day downright eventful. You're the first proper woman I ever spent a whole day with.'

That caused Stella to rise up on to

her elbows and stare at him. It was full dark, but he could feel the curious look on her face. 'Does that mean you only associate with dancehall girls or ladies of questionable morals?'

Brett laughed at the idea. 'At the end of a cattle drive, I often let loose the same as the other drovers, spending both time and money in a casino or saloon. I frequently danced with the gals and would buy 'em drinks, but I never did cotton to the idea of paying for more personal favors.'

'I thought most men enjoyed having fun with a loose woman.'

'Maybe,' he allowed, 'but I was raised to think love is more important than having a good time.'

'Oh, yes, the high moral character Reggie spoke of. I remember.'

He laughed. 'Reggie likes to say things like that, but he's a man with a good heart himself. I remember him giving a down-on-his-luck farmer twenty dollars one time. It was every dime Reggie had. He did it so the guy could feed his family until harvest. He teases me for carrying a Bible, but he enjoys listening to me when I read.'

'So he's not quite the sinner he says he is.'

'Don't let on that I said anything,' Brett warned her. 'He likes to make people think he's a scoundrel.'

'Your sisters, are they all married?' she changed the topic.

'Yeah, I'm the only single member of the family. The older girls have kids, but my younger sister only got married a few months back. I haven't seen anyone from home in seven years.'

'You did say you were on your way home . . . before you stumbled on to the murders.'

'Yes, my dad is wanting to retire. He wrote and asked if I'd take over the chore of running the ranch for him. Soon as we settle with Chilly and the others, Reggie and I will head on up to the ranch.'

'I guess I made everything harder for you.'

'Things will work out,' he told her. 'Once we tend to this pack of coyotes, we'll be on our way. And you'll be free to go and do whatever you want.'

Stella lay back down and was silent.

Brett wondered how much abuse and mistreatment the woman had endured at the hands of the men in her life. He had seen a couple blowhards who treated their wives like slaves, and he knew some men sometimes raised a hand to their wives. It grated on his conscience that a women should ever fear her husband, a man who was supposed to protect and cherish her. Marriage was supposed to be a union, a commitment to —

'Good night, Mr Jackson,' Stella murmured, the interruption startling him.

He managed a barely audible response, 'Uh, yeah, g'night, Mrs Burdette.' Then he closed his eyes. Sleep was something he hadn't gotten much of since he and Reggie's lives had been turned upside down by Stella's arrival. With luck, he would be able to collapse in a dreamless slumber and forget all about the rather attractive woman lying next to him.

His dominant male inclination responded with, '*Wanna bet!*'

7

Skinny moved over next to Long Tooth, peering hard at the dark form of the dead horse. He blinked and rubbed his eyes, then looked again.

'For the love of — He ain't there!' he exclaimed.

Long Tooth snorted. ''Course he's there. I been watching all damn night. He couldn't a left, less'n he dug himself a hole and burrowed away like a mole.'

'Well, I don't see nothing but the dead horse.'

Long Tooth stared into the dawn, wishing the light was a little better. 'Be full daylight soon and we'll spot him. He might have pulled some dirt over himself to try and hide.'

'We best get our horses, pard. If that jackal is on the hoof, we need to get after him right quick.'

'I tell yuh, he couldn't have got away!'

'Then where is he?'

'Give the sun a couple minutes more, till we can see good.'

But Skinny could see well enough. 'He's either burrowed under the dirt or he's sneaked out on us. I'm going down there and look for tracks.'

'We'll go together,' Long Tooth vowed. 'And we'll slip in nice and close with our guns ready.'

They readied their guns and started a wary approach down the slope. It seemed impossible that anyone could have escaped without being seen. The horse was slightly bloated in death, but the man was not in sight.

'You must have dozed off,' Skinny told Long Tooth. 'Ain't no way that guy could have crawled away without being seen.'

'I tell you, I never took my eyes off'n him and his dead horse, not once until you come back and relieved me for a spell. Could be you missed seeing him

158

make his escape.'

Drawing closer, they began to search the ground for sign. Skinny was fifty feet from the horse when he stopped and pointed.

'Look there, beneath the back hoofs and tail,' he said. 'Is that a mound of dirt?'

Long Tooth took a step closer, staring hard at the spot. 'Appears to be something there, buried under the sand, but it ain't no man. What the hell do you — ?'

The belly of the horse suddenly seemed to explode! A man's arm thrust out from the opening and a pistol opened fire!

Skinny took a bullet in the chest and another in the stomach. Long Tooth reacted late, swinging his gun around.

A slug tore through his abdomen and ruined his shot. The bullet from his buffalo gun kicked up the dirt a mere ten feet in front of him. Before he could grab for his pistol, he was hit a second time an inch below his right eye. In less time than it took to sneeze, both men were knocked to the ground, felled like the buffalo they had been slaughtering.

Reggie uncurled his legs as he pushed himself out of his hiding place. He was glad he had not left his poncho with Brett and the woman; wrapped about his head and shoulders, the rain slicker was covered with blood. He shrugged out of the poncho and recovered his hat from under Sally's neck. It took a moment or two before he could unkink his legs and rise to a standing position. Hiding in the hollowed out belly of a horse for several hours was not something he ever wanted to do again.

'You were about to figure it out,' Reggie spoke to the two dead men. 'You saw where I had stashed and covered Sally's innards. If you'd have been one second smarter, I would be as dead as my horse.'

He took a moment to check on the two hunters. There wasn't time to bury them, as he was already a day late for getting the help Brett and the lady were counting on. He looked off in the distance and wondered if they would be able to stay ahead of the hunters until tomorrow night.

He could take one of the hunter's horses and ride for Rimrock, but help would be delayed for at least one extra day. That meant Brett would be out of time. Plus, killing two of their number could change the hunter's plans. They might decide to run and get out of the territory before any organized pursuit could be mounted. It was a tough decision to make because he didn't know anything about his enemies.

Reggie began to walk up the incline, heading for the hunters' two horses. If he went for help, Brett and the woman might be killed. If he tried to reach them with an extra horse, there was a good chance he might run into more of the hunters and get himself killed.

'I'm guessing this is how I'm going to repay my debt to you, Yank,' Reggie grumbled under his breath. 'We will most likely die together.'

161

Rob was on the ground poking around. After a few minutes, and having followed a number of different tracks, he came back to his horse.

'Well?' Lionel asked.

'It looks like Stella walked in on two men. I read two distinct boot prints and there were two horses. I'd bet my favorite teeth one of those is the horse and rider Skinny and Long Tooth stopped.' He gave a wave of his arm. 'Rode off toward Rimrock, pretty much in a straight line.'

'And the woman?'

'The other horse went across the stream. There's a few things stashed in the brush. Something has been at it — coyote or some magpies, I'd guess — but I found a little food, a coffee pot and some personal stuff. They obviously lightened the load for the horse.'

'Riding double,' Chilly ventured. 'That makes sense.'

'One of them went for help and the

other is trying to keep us from finding the cook,' Lionel summed up.

'Why didn't all three of them make a run for Rimrock?' Max wondered aloud.

'Because we would have caught them out in the open — just like Skinny and Long Tooth did the lone rider,' Lionel informed his son. 'They probably figured one man wouldn't draw any attention. The plan might have worked, except Long Tooth found Stella's tracks and realized the rider had to have met up with her.'

'Good thing Long Tooth was the one to cut his trail,' Rob praised. 'He always did read sign like an Indian.'

'What now?' Max asked.

'The four of us will go after this second guy and the cook. Sonny and Sawyer are watching the camp, so the cook and her new friend can't sneak in and get another horse or any supplies.'

'And riding double, they couldn't have taken much with them to get by,' Chilly offered. 'The help they are expecting won't be showing up, so we can take our time and run them to ground.'

'Shouldn't we get some supplies, so we don't have to break off the chase?' Rob wanted to know.

Lionel gave a negative shake of his head. 'Their plan will be to get closer to wherever they expect help to come from — probably a posse from Rimrock — or to meet at a specified location. I doubt they intend to go any further north.'

'What you're saying, Big Daddy, is they will work a circle pattern or zigzag through the hills to keep ahead of us,' Chilly deduced.

'That's right, and we'll probably end up within a few miles of our base camp tonight, so one of us can return to get the supplies we need.'

'It's rugged terrain over along the mountain range,' Rob said. 'They are going to be on foot a good deal of the time if they want to save the horse.'

'True enough,' Chilly spoke up again, 'but they have a full day's head start.'

Max uttered a mirthless laugh. 'They expect help to be here by tomorrow sometime . . . and no one is coming.'

'Lead off, Rob,' Lionel ordered. 'Let's see how far and fast they can run.'

*   *   *

Trixie was a good horse, but she was worn down from packing double and entering the foothills the day before. Soon Brett and Stella were walking every half hour and leading the horse. Worse, there was no hard pack or rock plateaus, no beaten trails that would hide a horse's tracks. They needed to keep away from the hunters for two full days and that was beginning to look highly improbable.

They stopped for a breather beneath the shadow of a juniper tree and Brett allowed Trixie to munch on a little grass and antelope brush. While Stella sat down to recoup her strength, Brett walked up the hill to get a better view of

165

the lay of the land. It was rugged
territory higher up, yet dangerous to
stay so low. After a few minutes, he
walked back down to the woman and
his horse.

'This is so unfair for you,' Stella
spoke up upon his return. 'You could
have easily avoided the hunters without
me.'

'Don't forget, Reggie and I came
after them on our own. We would have
still had to think up a plan to catch
them.'

'Yes, but you could have sent for the
army right away and set a trap for them
while they were all off hunting. It would
have been no trouble at all to arrest
them at the camp.'

'The end result will be the same,' he
tossed off her thinking. 'We'll get them.'

'Not if I keep holding you back. You
would be smart to leave me on my own.
You could escape and meet Reggie,
then — '

'No.'

She frowned. 'I'm nothing to you.

Why are you risking your life and even the mission you're on just to keep dragging me along?'

'Because you are not *nothing* to me and you need our help.'

She glowered at him. 'You're so . . . so high and mighty! You can't possibly think you're going to save me?' She laughed her contempt. 'We might stay ahead of those men for the rest of today but they'll have us by tomorrow. These are not ordinary men, they are a bunch of bloodhounds. One was a scout for the army and they are all professional hunters! You not only won't prevent them from killing me, but you'll be killed yourself. What kind of strategy is that?'

'I'm a fair shot with a rifle, ma'am. If they get too close, I'll do whatever it takes to stop them.'

'They have buffalo guns, Mr Jackson, and I've listened to their bragging about some of the impossible shots they've made. They can shoot at you from a distance so far away that you won't be able to shoot back, and they've been practicing on buffalo for the last few weeks.'

'It's different up here in the hills,' he argued. 'If we stick to the high ground, with them below us, their guns will be little better than mine. They are also used to shooting on a level plain, not straight up or down a mountainside.' He grunted cynically, 'And, lastly, buffalo don't shoot back.'

'Yes, but there are eight of them!'

Brett sighed. 'Look, ma'am, I'm going to do the best I can to stay alive and keep you that way too. I won't give up without a fight and I'm not going to leave you behind. If you sneak off in the night and surrender to them, you will be sacrificing your life for no reason. Those filthy vermin are going to pay for killing the Hannigans, and your brother-in-law too. Whatever happens, I'm going to see those men dead or in prison.'

'You're a proud and stubborn man,' she said tightly. 'But you are flesh and blood. You can die as easily as anyone else.'

Brett became wistful, as if touched by her words. When he spoke, it was in a calm voice, little more than a whisper.

'Twice during the war, the man walking next to me was killed by a Confederate bullet. During a calvary charge, shrapnel from a cannon knocked down the horses and men on either side of me, yet I rode off of the battlefield without a scratch.' Brett shook his head. 'When I left the army, I had a gut feeling and rode off of the usual trail in Indian country. Instead of me ending up dying from having a fire built on my chest, I was able to save Reggie from that very fate.' He took a breath, still in awe of how many times death had come close without him suffering any harm.

'While on our last cattle drive, a rattlesnake slithered into one of the bedrolls during the night. That man died the following day from several bites. His bed was next to mine.' He put on a hard expression. 'I don't pray as much as I should, but I've always tried to do what I thought was right. Now, whether that means God has been looking out for me, I can't really say. But someone seems to have watched over me all these years. And I'm guessing that someone is not real pleased at the actions of these hunters.'

He paused to look down the mountain, knowing the killers were on their trail and drawing closer. 'I'm going to stop Chilly and the others from hurting anyone else ever again.' He flicked a glance at her. Stella had a puzzled expression on her face, as if trying to decide if he was crazy, possessed, or even deluded into thinking he was embodied with a charmed life. He dismissed the look. 'That includes you too, Mrs Burdette.'

Stella struggled to her feet. Stiff and sore, she uttered an unfeminine grunt from the effort. The look she gave him had changed from defeat to determination.

'All right, you deluded, self-righteous fanatic.' She said the words critically, yet there was a slight lift at the corners of her mouth. 'If you're too dumb to listen to reason, I guess I've no choice but to go along with your insanity.'

Brett went to the horse and waited for her to join him. 'You ride in the saddle for a bit,' he said. 'I'll lead Trixie for the next little while.'

'I'm no more tired than you are,' she objected.

'The going is pretty rough until we get over the next hill. I'll ride when we reach the basin.'

She pulled a face to show her displeasure, but attempted to lift her leg high enough to get her foot in the stirrup. Standing on a mild slope, she lost her balance. Luckily, Brett caught her under the arms before she fell. He lifted enough to help her to stand back up, maintaining his hold to keep her steady.

'I . . . I'm stiffer than I thought,' she said, obviously embarrassed.

'Let me give you a hand,' Brett suggested.

Stella pivoted to face him. Unexpectedly, she gazed into his eyes, remaining within his grasp. There was something wholly inviting about the situation, causing Brett to lose track of time and suspend his thought process.

'You seem such a fine woman, Mrs Burdette,' he said without thinking. 'I can't imagine any man ever raising a hand to you.'

A flash of surprise came into her face, followed at once by a slight tint of her cheeks. She quickly shielded her eyes by lowering her thick, lash-adorned lids. Instead of scalding his hide or insulting the entire male of the species, Stella appeared unsure of herself.

'Mr Jackson, I . . . ' she began haltingly. 'You shouldn't . . . ' Another awkward pause.

'I beg your pardon, ma'am,' Brett said. 'I didn't mean to make you uncomfortable. I know how you feel about us men.'

The statement caused her expression to become defensive. 'No,' she said, making eye contact. 'I can see you and Reggie are decent and caring. I've been wrong to lump you in with the other men in my life.'

Brett enjoyed the depth of her gaze, the rich brown of her eyes, and something more, something he had not seen before. It was fleeting, a mere shadow that floated across her face like a passing cloud, but he recognized it; Stella had been unable to hide the minute demure flush.

Rather than make things more awkward and maybe do something rash, he carefully stepped back alongside the horse and locked his hands together below his waist. Bending slightly, he instructed her.

'Place your left knee into my hands, then lean forward and reach for the saddle.'

Stella wavered only a second, then did as he told her. With her knee firmly in his hands, she shifted her weight and took hold of the saddle. He lifted her upward and she easily swung her leg over the saddle and slid into place.

Brett didn't say anything more. He took the reins and began to lead Trixie along the hogback ridge, making for the hill's summit. He knew what lay on the other side, having seen it from his walk up the slope.

Throwing a look over his shoulder, he scanned the foothills below. He couldn't see anything moving yet, but the hunters would be coming. He wondered when they had found his and Reggie's camp. Did they send someone after Reggie? Had they crossed the creek at once and taken up the pursuit immediately? If they had, they might be within a mile or two and closing in on him and Stella. He might glimpse them on his back trail at any moment.

He shook away the worries. The only option for him was to keep moving and hope they could elude the hunters until the next afternoon. If Reggie didn't arrive in time, he would have to face them alone; it was not a comforting thought.

★ ★ ★

Sundown found Reggie overlooking the hunters' camp. The chuck wagon and two large tents were in place. He kept to the higher sagebrush and waited until he was certain there were only two men in camp. After they had prepared some kind of stew and sat down to eat, he made his move.

Both had plates on their laps and were sitting with their legs crossed. It was an impossible position from which to draw a gun. Reggie walked right in on them with his own gun ready.

'Howdy, boys,' he spoke up, cocking the pistol menacingly.

The one raised his hands, while the other held a spoonful of food inches from his mouth. He froze in that position.

'Be so kind as to tell me your names.'

'Whata yuh want?' the one with the spoon asked.

'Is that your given name, *Whatayawant?*' Reggie queried. 'If so, I've got to ask, what country do you come from, fella?'

'I'm Sawyer,' the man whose hands were up replied. 'This is Sonny, my older brother.'

'A couple of the Kenton boys, huh?' Reggie spat out the words. 'You'd be two of the mangy critters who killed the people at that trading post.'

'No!' Sawyer cried, his eyes wide and a sinfully guilty look washing across his face. 'I mean, it was an accident!'

'And the mistreatment of that poor little girl, before you killed her, was that an accident too?'

Sonny lowered the fork to the plate and slipped the tin from his lap to the ground. 'Who are you mister and what do you want?'

'I'm what you might call a righteous vigilante, Sonny. You did an evil deed and I'm here to collect payment.'

'You a lawman?' Sawyer asked.

'My badge is my Colt .45 and I'm going to do whatever the hell I feel is necessary in order to see that justice is done.' Reggie took a quick glance around. 'All of the others from camp are out chasing after the cook?'

Sawyer looked sick. 'Yes.'

'I stayed to tend my brother, cause he don't have the innards to be a man,' Sonny sneered.

'Just 'cause I didn't take part in the killing,' Sawyer whined. 'Everyone thinks I'm a coward or something.'

Reggie recalled Stella saying she thought Sawyer was the only innocent man in the lot. He asked the young man, 'What if I was to ask you to get a horse and ride for Texas or some other far away place? Would you go?'

'What kind of game are you playing, mister?' Sonny wanted to know, before his brother had time for a reply.

'Well, I happen to believe your brother is telling the truth, Sonny. You and the others killed that old man, his wife and daughter. But I can believe

Sawyer didn't want any part of it.'

'And what about me?'

Reggie showed a menacing grin. 'You're going to die for what you did, Sonny. Don't you have no doubt about it.'

Sonny looked at Sawyer. 'We can take him together, you and me. Give me some help here.'

Sawyer shook his head. 'I'm sick to death about what you and the others did, Sonny. I can still hear that girl sobbing, crying for her mom and dad. Damn it all, Sonny, I can't even close my eyes at night!'

'I told Pa you didn't have an ounce of guts.'

'What's it gonna be, Sonny?' Reggie asked, easing the hammer back into place and sliding his gun into its holster. 'You want to try your luck with a judge and jury, or do you want to slap leather and see if you're going to live or die right here tonight?'

Sonny placed his right hand on the ground, pretending he was going to get to his feet. 'Soon as I get up, we'll see just how fast you are,' he said.

But instead of trying to stand, he grabbed the handle of his pistol and tried to yank it free!

The single gunshot sounded like a cannon in the night.

Sonny flopped on to his back with a bullet in his heart. He rolled his head to one side, a final look at Sawyer, but the sight had left his eyes and he lay still.

Sawyer stared down at him in horror, then put a grave look on Reggie. 'I knew we'd all die for what happened at the trading post,' he lamented, tears glistening in his eyes. 'And then Chilly killed Stella's brother-in-law. Skinny rode in last night and said he and Long Tooth were going to kill another man today.' He sniffed against the tears. 'I tried to get Pa to leave, but he wouldn't go. He feels responsible, because Sonny and Max were both in on the killings and he didn't try to stop them.'

'Skinny and Long Tooth have paid the price for their sins,' Reggie informed him. 'So has Sonny. Now it's time for me to deal with you.'

Sawyer took a breath and waited, his teeth clenched to maintain his courage. 'I won't draw against you; I only ask for you to make it quick.'

Reggie didn't shoot. He said, 'Tell me what's happening with the other hunters.'

'We expected Skinny and Long Tooth back before now,' the young man answered. 'As for the others, Max stopped by and got some supplies a couple hours back. He said they were on the trail of the cook and another guy.' He arched his brow. 'Friend of yours?'

Reggie didn't answer his question. 'So they aren't coming back here tonight?'

'No, they don't want to get too far from the trail they are following. Max said they would run them down sometime tomorrow, because they were riding double.'

Reggie felt the boy was telling him

the truth. He holstered his gun and nodded in the direction of the freight wagon. 'I see you have some buffalo hides and meat ready to go.'

'We picked up the stuff in the freight wagon today,' Sawyer replied. 'If something went wrong, we were to be ready to head for Rimrock.'

'Looks like a man would make enough on a load like that to get you a fresh start somewhere.'

Sawyer frowned. 'You're not going to let me go?'

'I'm not anxious to kill a man whose only crime was being unable to stand up against his family. Mrs Burdette vouched for you. She said she didn't think you were involved in the murders, and Sonny basically said the same thing. I'm going to let you hitch a team to that wagon of hides and head for the railhead. If you're smart, you'll never look back.'

'You're asking me to desert my family.'

'No, I'm giving you a choice,' Reggie

corrected, resting his hand on the butt of his pistol. 'You can take the wagon and start a new life, without your pa and brothers, or you can choose to die with them. If you decide the latter, I'll kill you here and now. What's it going to be?'

'I'd like to bury Sonny first,' Sawyer said quietly. 'There's room over where we covered the body of Mr Burdette.'

Reggie sighed, resigning himself to remaining at the camp until morning. 'I'll take his feet, you get his arms and lead the way.'

8

'What's that?' Lionel growled at Max, as he off-loaded the supplies from the back of his horse. 'Skinny and Long Tooth didn't get back to camp yet?'

'Nary a sign of them, Pa,' Max replied. 'Sonny said they hadn't seen a soul all day. They might have missed the two of them when they went out to pick up the load of hides, but that sure don't explain where they're at.'

'It don't make sense,' Chilly spoke up. 'Skinny said they were only about eight or ten miles from camp. He and Long Tooth were supposed to kill that *hombre* they had pinned down at sunup.'

'Maybe the guy put up a better fight than they figured,' Lionel surmised. 'Could be he even wounded one of them. Might have killed one of their horses or something. A good many things could be keeping them from getting back.'

'I'll bet they are back at camp by this time,' Rob said. 'They probably got in late and decided to wait until morning to come join us.' He shrugged. 'Why sleep on the cold damp ground when the tent is handy.'

'Yeah, I told Sonny our whereabouts,' Max agreed with the logic. 'I'd wager they stuck around for a hot meal and a decent night's sleep.'

'I'm sure they'll be along tomorrow. And once we see where this guy is headed, we'll split up and trap him between us.'

'Well, I'll be glad when this is over,' Rob said. 'And I don't blame Skinny and Long Tooth for waiting till morning to join us. That tent wasn't the most comfortable place to sleep, but it sure beats bunking under the stars. It's going to be another cold night.'

★ ★ ★

Stella seemed reserved and had not spoken much all afternoon. After the sun went down, Brett began to look for a place to spend the night. He followed a ravine and discovered a rocky pocket where some water had collected. It was not much, but it would take care of the horse and he had filled the canteen at another small reservoir during the afternoon.

'We won't dare start a fire tonight,' he told Stella, as he guided the horse down next to the natural pool. 'They shouldn't catch up with us until tomorrow, but we can't take the chance one of them is out there tonight. If they guess our direction and have an experienced tracker, one or more of them might circle down on the flatlands to get out in front of us.'

She didn't offer an opinion and Brett swung his leg over the pommel and dismounted by sliding down. He turned toward her and reached up to help her down. As they had done a great deal of walking and then riding during the day,

Stella had gotten used to his helping hand. While she had seemed indifferent and reserved the first time or two, she actually appeared to welcome the contact this time. When he eased her to the ground, she stood within his grasp, making no effort to move away.

The way she looked at him caused him to ask, 'What is it?'

'I was thinking what a genuinely nice person you are,' she said boldly.

Brett about laughed, but realized she was being completely serious. 'That's quite a jump, from being a worthless, no-good man to a nice person.'

'You're making fun of me,' she complained. 'But it's not something that's easy for me to admit. I've never really been around a gentleman before . . . not for any length of time.' With a timid smile, 'I had begun to think such men didn't really exsist.'

Brett reciprocated, 'And, although you were a might hostile at the beginning, I admit that I find you a very attractive and special lady.'

A flush rose in Stella's cheeks, but she made no offer to move, continuing to stand close. Brett leaned slightly toward her and tilted his head. He expected her to pull back, to duck to turn away . . . but she allowed him to kiss her ever so gently on the lips. He lingered only a few delightful moments before he drew back.

Stella's eyes remained closed for a second or two, then the lashes fluttered and she regarded him with a most peculiar expression. He thought he'd made a mess of kissing her until a slight smile came on to her lips.

'Whatever is in your pocket?' she asked.

Brett might have thought she would mention how his kissing her was impetuous or a brash move, something about impertinence or taking advantage of her. At the unexpected question, he swallowed his confusion and forced his brain to work.

'Uh, I started carrying a Bible with me during the war. It gave me comfort when times were bad.' He shrugged. 'Plus, if I were killed, I thought it might help to save my soul.'

Another fleeting smile played along her inviting lips. 'It will be a shame being hunted down and killed tomorrow. I would have enjoyed getting to know you better, Mr Jackson.'

'My thoughts as well, Mrs Burdette.'

'Estelle,' she corrected. 'I ... I've always wished I was fond enough of a man to have him call me that.'

Brett grinned. 'I'd be privileged to have that honor ... *Estelle*. And I prefer Brett to Mr Jackson, stupid, worthless man, or idiot male.'

She uttered an unrestrained laugh at his comment ... and it sounded beautiful.

* * *

Rob topped the rise and made a grab for his Sharps buffalo gun. He was too slow, so he stopped his horse and waited for the others to catch up.

'They just went over the ridge,' he informed Lionel, pointing to the place. 'A few seconds sooner and I'd have had a clear shot at them.'

'Them? Two of them like we thought, a man and Stella?'

'Yep. I'd guess we're a quarter mile or so behind, but we have to cross this gully so it means we're not going to gain much ground in the next little while.'

Lionel looked to where he indicated the riders had gone and studied the terrain. The ridge indicated was one of two legs of twin mountainous ravines he had noticed when they began to climb this lower range. Tracking the landscape higher up, the two ravines came together at a rocky butte. There was a shell-rock face towering upwards and the wall appeared to span the junction of both summits, limiting any access to the mountain range beyond. After a short time he tipped his head toward the peak.

'I'll bet the guy is going to hole up

there at the foot of that stone escarpment, where the two ravines meet. It's the best place for miles around to make a stand.'

'Be impossible to attack from directly below,' Rob said, considering his conclusion. 'I'll bet a sizable waterfall comes down from that shelf after a heavy rain. It looks to drop a hundred feet or more. That means their only exit is down one of the two ridges.'

Lionel grinned. 'We've got them!'

'A lot of cover up there in those rocks.'

'Yes, but our brave knight thinks he has help on the way. The man Long Tooth and Skinny cut down didn't make it.'

Max said, 'Speaking of those two, I wonder why they haven't caught up with us yet.'

'It doesn't matter, Son,' Lionel informed him confidently. 'If we split up we can gain control of both ravines. The man and our cook will be trapped.'

'If he burrows into those rocks, it

could be a real chore to get at him,' Rob observed. 'However, we can sure enough make his life miserable. While there's good cover, a good many bullets will ricochet or send pieces of rock flying in every direction. We can pepper his hide until he makes a mistake.'

Lionel looked at the different routes leading down through the gully. 'When we reach the bottom of the wash, you and Chilly can follow it out. You swing around the lower foothills and get to that far ravine. While you two come up that way, Max and I will cross over on this upper route and stay on their trail. If the guy doesn't make a stand at the rocky base of that sheer cliff we'll still have him trapped between us.'

'We don't know how good he is with a rifle, Big Daddy,' Chilly warned. 'Best approach him carefully.'

'I agree. When we get within rifle range, we'll stay close to the trees and not get out in the open. Once we're sure Stella and her pal have stopped to make a stand, we will move in on foot.'

He gave a sharp look at Rob. 'You two will have to ride hard to prevent them from going down the other side.'

'We shouldn't have any trouble getting ahead of them,' Rob agreed with the plan. 'Once we hit the bottom of the gully, we can turn our horses loose and make a direct line for that second ravine. We should be able to get near the top of the ridge before they can cross that rocky point and start down.'

'Let's get moving. With any luck, we'll end this before dark and head back to camp.'

Rob and Chilly immediately put their mounts down the steep slope, working around the tangle of brush and the few trees, hurrying to reach the bottom of the wash.

After watching them for a bit, Lionel looked over at his son. 'You and I will take our time following the tracks. With luck, the guy and Stella will keep running and head down the other way. I'd just as soon Chilly had the woman's death on his conscience.'

'Chilly is a lot of fun to be around, Pa,' Max said, 'but I'm the first to admit he's about the most crazy cuss I ever met.'

'When I asked Rob to come along, I didn't know much about his brother. We only had to rob that trading post and be gone. Once Chilly shot the old man . . . ' Lionel sighed. 'Then he up and kills that harmless old coot in camp. Couldn't keep his damned hands off of Stella until we had at least finished with the hunt.'

'Struck me a dumb thing to do too. It ain't like the cook is anything special,' Max said. 'I mean, she ain't hard to look at, but she's got a tongue that could rip bark from a tree.'

'Most hateful woman I ever met, but she was a good cook.'

'Yeah, she did serve up good tasting grub.'

Lionel took a look down the hillside. 'They are at the bottom of the wash. We'd best get after the cook. If we keep up the pressure, the guy she's riding with might just not be looking for Chilly and Rob to be in his path.'

'I hear you, Pa. Let's get after them.'

★　★　★

Brett pushed Trixie hard until they reached the rocky shelf and the jagged stone escarpment. The wall above wasn't all that high above the ledge — less than a hundred feet — but it breeched the way for passage into the higher mountains from both ravines. The only way down was the way they had come unless they took the second ridge and followed it to a point where they could descend its slope.

Stopping his mount, Brett swung his leg over the pommel and slid down to the ground. Estelle was ready when he reached for her and came easily down at his side.

'What do you see?' she asked, when Brett paused to stare hard along their back trail.

'They've reached the hogback ridge

and are coming pretty fast. I didn't plan on them being so close.'

'Can we stay ahead of them?'

Brett shook his head. 'This is where I told Reggie we would be — Devil's Fork, we named it. There's good cover here.'

'But there might be all eight men after us!'

'A couple probably stuck close to the camp to make sure we didn't steal another horse or retrieve your belongings.'

'Well then, that's different,' she said with a trace of humor entering her serious tone of voice. 'With only six of them, we've nothing to worry about.'

He grinned at her. 'Just what I was thinking.'

Estelle looked around. 'The horse might be safer if we move her over beneath that overhang.'

Brett surveyed their position. 'I agree, although this rock facing will cause a lot of rock chips when the bullets start to fly.' He walked around and looked down the sheer precipice. 'They won't be coming from above, because of the overhang and it's a straight drop down for over a hundred feet. That means they can only come from the rim of either ravine.'

Estelle said nothing, waiting for him to decide the best way to defend their position.

There were several large boulders, but the terrace they were on was a couple hundred feet across. It didn't allow for him to cover both sides at once. He had his Winchester and a pistol, but the handgun was pretty useless until it came to close range shooting. He could stop the approach of the hunters following him, but they would certainly send someone to come up the other side. They might have done that already to cut them off.

The thought was still in his mind when he spotted two riders off in the distant trees of the second ravine. The hand was dealt. With hunters both ahead and behind them, this was where they would have to make their fight.

'Can you load and shoot a gun?' he asked Estelle.

'Myron taught me a little, in case of Indians, because we sometimes stayed in an empty shack or cabin a long way from the nearest town. I can't hit anything very far away, but I can make some noise.'

Brett emptied his gun and handed her the shells, then he instructed her to load his pistol. Once she was successful, he did the same thing again. She did the chore a little quicker this time.

'All right,' he praised her efforts, 'You've got it.'

'What do you want me to do?'

He smiled at the offer. 'See? That's the way a man and a woman make a life together. They depend on one another; they work together.'

'I think we can *depend* on both getting killed *together*.'

In spite of the dire situation, he laughed and admitted, 'Probably.'

Then they got to work, putting Trixie

where she was protected by the natural concave features of the cliff. He handed Estelle the extra bullets to his handgun and gave her the canteen.

'You stay down behind these rocks,' he instructed. 'I'll try to knock down one or two of the men coming up our left flank. Then I'm going to move so I can be ready for the men following us. When I cross to the right side, you come up to where you can watch the left. A shot now and again is all it should take to keep them at bay.'

Estelle was visibly trembling with fright, but she gave a solemn nod of understanding.

'You don't have to raise up and show yourself,' he said. 'Just take a quick peek around the rocks — choose a different spot each time — and see that they aren't moving in on us.'

'I shoot at them but don't risk getting shot myself,' she clarified.

'Yes, and be sure to count your shots. Reload each time you've emptied the gun. If you get down to the last ten rounds, stop firing and signal me.'

'What will we do then?'

'Our plan is to hold until dark. Reggie should be here by then. If not, we'll fall back and take up a position by the horse.'

He looked at her for a moment, wishing there was more time. Instead of trying to find the right thing to say, he pulled her into his arms and kissed her. Whether it was fear or if she had decided this was a man she could trust, Estelle kissed back. Then she clung to him for several seconds.

'We can do this,' Brett told her softly. 'Those men are the only thing in the way of our making the trip to my folks' ranch and starting a life together. I'm going to fight like hell to see we get that chance.'

Estelle gazed up at him and smiled. 'Yes, we'll both fight like hell to get that chance.'

Brett chuckled at her spunk. 'Never heard a proper lady use a profanity before.'

'I suppose you think less of me for it?'

He kissed her again and said, 'Not when it's spoken for both our sakes.'

There was no more time. He released her from his embrace and grabbed up his rifle. Keeping low, he crept over to the outcropping boulders and found a good place to keep watch. He motioned to Estelle, so she would know it was the position he wanted her to move to when he crossed back to watch their back trail.

Estelle gave an affirmative nod and ducked in next to Trixie. She had the gun out, the bullets tucked into her jacket pocket, and was ready to face whatever fate was in store for them.

9

Rob slowed as they climbed toward the summit, trying to get a look at the landscape ahead. He knew they were nearing the junction where the two ravines met. He moved into a clearing and tried to see across the deep gorge but there were too many trees.

'We should have run into the cook and her pal by this time,' he said to Chilly. 'If they stopped up at that rock mesa, Lionel and Max should have caught up to them by now. We should have heard shooting.'

'I think Big Daddy wants us to do the dirty work,' Chilly sneered. 'You remember he didn't do much at the trading post.'

Rob looked over at his brother. 'Not everyone has it in them to kill people, Chilly. I didn't shoot that old man or the woman either.'

Chilly guffawed. 'Yeah, but you have me along for the dirty work. You don't need to even pack a gun, except to kill buffalo.'

'Sawyer was right about one thing. I have to believe you'll be the death of me.'

'Who wants to live forever?' Chilly asked. 'Better to make your own rules and have fun while you can.'

Rob sat up straight. 'That's sure enough the way you've always lived. I guess I shouldn't think — '

The bullet hit Rob with the impact of someone swinging a sixteen pound hammer. Even as the shot rang out and echoed down the valley, Rob spilled from his saddle and landed on the ground in a twisted heap.

Chilly ducked instantly, jumped down from his horse and hurried over to where Rob had fallen. He quickly dragged him to cover within the brush and trees so that the shooter couldn't get in a second shot. It was only random chance that Rob had been sitting out in the small clearing instead of Chilly.

Rob's eyes were open wide, his face contorted in pain and shock.

'Rob!' Chilly cried, kneeling over his body. 'Hang on, big brother, I'll get something for a bandage. You'll be all right.'

But Rob slowly rolled his head from side to side. 'It's like I said, Chilly . . . ' he coughed and blood trickled from his mouth. 'You'll be . . . death . . . of me,' he whispered hoarsely. A final, haggard sigh of air escaped through his mouth and he was dead.

Chilly rose up, filled with a hateful fury. The rage nearly cost him his life. A bullet tore through the top of his hat and knocked it from his head. It was enough to remind him to be a little more cautious.

'I'll pay back that interfering son for you, Rob,' he vowed. 'You ain't going to your grave alone!'

Retrieving his hat, he kept low and began to work his way along the side of the hill. He had to use the trees and brush as cover. It slowed his approach, but he swore to kill the man who had shot his brother.

* ★ *

Brett had gotten a good bead on the first rider. He felt certain the bullet had eliminated one of the hunters from the fight. The second shot was to make the other one or two coming from that direction think he was still holding his position. With a wave to Estelle, he backed away from his cover and began to run for the other side.

He sprinted across the open ground, but something hit him high in the leg and he sprawled headlong on to the hard ground. He kept hold of his rifle and crawled for the cover of his second chosen stronghold. By the time he reached the safety of the boulders several more shots had been fired at him from the right flank.

His lower thigh burned and blood began to soak through his trousers. He used his bandanna to wrap about the wound to stem the bleeding. Then he peeked quickly between two rocks looking for the gunmen.

A bullet sang off of the top of the stone and he pulled back. He hadn't been able to tell how many men there were. He figured only one or two were over on Estelle's side. If a couple men remained back at the wagon, that would leave either three or four who were shooting from this side. It wasn't logical to think he could defeat five men at once, attacking from two different directions. But he had no choice. They had to hold out until help arrived.

Estelle had been moving to take up her firing position when Brett went down so she didn't know he had been hit. She was now defending the left side of their stronghold. He glanced over as she took a quick peek around the rocks. Pulling back at once, she then poked her gun around a boulder and fired off a single round in the direction of the hunters. As if she knew Brett would be watching her, she looked over at him and gave a bit of a wave to show she was following the plan.

Brett encouraged her with a lifted hand of his own, then turned his attention back to the hunters who were attacking his position. Listening to the sounds of the guns he identified only two firing. That was puzzling. Where were the other hunters? He had spotted only two moving in the trees on the opposite side, and one of those was out of the fight. There had to be more of them he couldn't see, either on one ridge or the other; they just hadn't started shooting yet.

Scooting to a new position, he removed his hat and took a quick glance. He thought he saw movement, but didn't dare risk exposing himself for more than a second or two at a time. If they got him, Estelle would be at their mercy . . . something the hunter named Chilly wasn't known for.

Another couple rounds screamed off the boulders, one ricocheting off the cliff façade behind him. He readied his rifle, set his weight on his good leg and rose up. He didn't have time to take aim, but he fired off a round in the direction of the attackers. Ducking for cover, two more bullets whined off of his stone fortress.

The men moving forward would be able to work together, one shooting and one moving. They could each take up a position to watch one side of his protective wall. Then, no matter which side he chose, one of them would have a shot at him. Searching for options, he heard Estelle fire again.

If they retreated to where the horse was, they would be trapped without an escape route. Once pinned under the overhang, the hunters could shower them with lead until one of the bullets scored a hit, even if it was a ricochet. It was a last refuge, but it offered no real hope of staying alive.

Suddenly, Estelle fired again and again. Brett whirled about to see what was happening and she shot twice more. He could tell she had seen one of the hunters and was trying to drive him back. That meant time was running out.

Estelle began to reload the gun, while Brett had to return to the attackers on his side. They were firing now, blasting away until he couldn't raise his head. No doubt the hunters had decided on new positions and were moving. The end was drawing near.

Brett took a quick peek and nearly caught a slug in his teeth! The bullet chipped off a piece of rock not an inch over his head. He was on his knees and sought to move back to the other end of the outcrop of rocks. That's when he heard the warning: 'Brett! Look out!'

Even as he turned, he knew he was done. A hunter from the left flank had charged right past Estelle's position. He was thirty feet away — his handgun was pointed at Brett's chest. He fired two rapid shots . . .

It felt like being kicked in the chest by a mule . . . with both hoofs. Brett's vision was lost to an instant black curtain, his breath left his body and he went down on his back feeling nothing.

Far off in his mind, he heard shouting and vaguely recognized Estelle cursing. Then there came a steady roar of gunfire, one shot after another after another. Brett clung to consciousness, but he had no air in his lungs. He prayed Estelle would have a quick death and let the blackness take him.

★　★　★

Estelle kept pulling the trigger. She had been trying to reload when Chilly raced past her. Once she had bullets in the gun, she went after Chilly, walking toward him and firing at the same time, trying with all of her might to hit and kill the rabid beast. The first shot was lucky, striking his gun arm. But he was still standing when the hammer stuck an empty chamber and the next three pulls of the trigger also got nothing but harmless *clicks*.

Chilly swore vehemently at her, but, along with hitting his right wrist, a second bullet had buried itself in his left hip and a third had nicked his cheek. He made the effort to bend over and recover his pistol, but his left leg gave out. He staggered backward, slipped on the steep slope and his feet went out from under him. Landing on his stomach, he slid on the shale rock, his lower body going over the edge of the precipice. He grabbed wildly for a handhold, but he could only use his left hand. He managed to catch hold of a chunk of protruding rock with his fingers, saving him from dropping a hundred feet to his death. However, the gun was out of reach and he was helpless, dangling over the side of a cliff.

There came more shooting along their back trail, but Estelle cared about nothing but reaching Brett. She scrambled over to him and dropped to her knees. Sobbing, she lifted his head on to her lap.

'Don't die, Brett,' she cried. 'Please . . . I don't want you to leave me.'

A figure appeared around the boulders, but Estelle had not reloaded the pistol. She could only weep over Brett and look up to see which hunter would be the one to kill her.

'What the hell, woman?' Reggie wanted to know. 'Don't tell me you let them miserable vultures shoot the Yank?'

'I was reloading the gun,' she managed between sobs. 'Chilly got past me before I had any bullets.'

'Let me have a look,' Reggie said, his voice more gentle now. 'I've seen a good many wounds during the war. Maybe I can help.'

Estelle moved away so Reggie could kneel over his friend. She took that time to look around. She spied Chilly clinging to a piece of rock for dear life. His face was red from the strain of holding on, but he didn't have the strength to pull himself up.

'What about the other hunters?' she

asked, unable to comprehend how the fight could be over.

'I suspect the Yank managed to hit one of those jaspers. That only left three, and you took out Chilly. I sneaked up on the other two about the time Chilly came charging across the ledge.'

'But there were eight of them,' she murmured, still amazed to be alive.

'If that don't beat all!' Reggie exclaimed, standing up. 'I guess the Yank was right.'

Estelle scowled at his flippancy. 'About what?'

Brett was stirring and his eyes popped open. He took a breath and groaned. Estelle stared agape at Reggie.

'Looks like those fellows the Yank was always reading about come through for him after all.'

'I don't understand. What are you saying, Reggie?'

He held out the Bible Brett always carried in his jacket pocket. 'It would appear Mathew, Mark, Luke and John saved his life. The two bullets stopped before they went all the way through the book.'

'But the blood — '

'Is from his leg,' Reggie told her. 'I don't think it's too bad.'

Estelle sank down next to Brett as he sat up. The two of them hugged while Reggie walked over to check on Chilly.

The man's expression was a mask of hate and several blood veins looked ready to explode. Straining to hold on to the crease in the rock facing, his entire weight hung over the edge. He had his teeth set from the immense effort.

'You need a little help do you, Chilly?' Reggie asked. 'Thought you'd be eager to join up with your pals in hell.'

'Get me up from here,' he gasped. 'We've got a thousand dollars built up from our hides. Pull me up and it's yours.'

'Sorry to give you the bad news, but Sawyer is going to collect your money. I imagine it's in his hands by this time.'

'I . . . I can't hang on much longer,' Chilly complained.

Reggie put his foot on to the man's hand. Chilly grimaced when he applied pressure. 'There you go, pardner,' Reggie drawled. 'See how I'm helping you? Long as I have my foot on your paw, you don't have to worry about falling.'

'Come on, man. I never did anything to you personally.'

'Wa'al now, let's run up a tally and see if you're right,' Reggie replied. 'You killed that old man and his wife, then raped and killed their daughter.' He paused. 'You're right, that was personal to Brett, but not to me. Then you killed Mrs Burdette's brother-in-law.' Another pause. 'You're right again. That was personal to her, but not to me.' His voice grew ice cold. 'Then you shot the Yank twice in the heart — damn good shooting it was too.' He put his hands on his hips and glowered down at the ruthless animal called Chilly. 'That, my friend, I do take personal.' And he stepped back, removing his foot from Chilly's hand.

A deathly panicked look, a scream forming on his lips, and Chilly lost his hold and slipped out of sight. His agonized shriek was cut short when his body collided with the rocky basin below.

★   ★   ★

Brett had his wind back by the time Reggie returned.

'You cut the rescue pretty close, Reggie,' he said. 'I figured to never wake up.'

'Hell, Yank, I can't imagine what you would be worrying about, not with both me and the good Lord watching over you.'

Brett grinned and looked at Estelle. 'I told you that book could save my soul. Looks like it also saved my life.'

'Even your book couldn't have saved Chilly,' Reggie commented. 'I held on to him as long as I could, but I got a cramp in my big toe.'

'I would have preferred to see him hang,' Brett said.

Reggie bobbed his head. 'That would have been entertaining too, but I'm already saddled with a cripple and a love-sick woman. Besides which, Rimrock is a full day the wrong way. I've a mind to see that ranch of yours.'

'Me too,' Estelle joined in. 'And if I hadn't been such a horrible shot, I would have killed Chilly several times over myself.'

'So where is the help you were supposed to bring?' Brett wanted to know.

'I brung the three you needed most,' Reggie replied with a grin. 'Me, myself and I. Can't understand why you would need more than that.'

'You decided to come back alone?'

'Sally made the choice for me. I've a real story to tell you about how that horse saved my life.' He put a hard look on Brett. 'And I don't want you thinking it's one of those made up tales . . . the kind you often claim my *real life* stories are.'

'I can't wait,' Brett said drily.

'Well, I can,' Estelle stopped the chatter. 'We need to tend to Brett's leg and get these bodies taken care of. Then we have to ride back to the wagon to get my things.'

'Shucks, Estelle,' Brett spoke up. 'Anything you need, we'll buy at the store before we head out to the ranch.' He grew serious. 'I mean, unless you left something at the wagon that is of special value or has a personal attachment for you.'

The lady smiled. 'Now that you mention it, everything I've been looking for is right here . . . with you.'

Brett drew her close enough that he could kiss her.

'Wa'al that's just fine,' Reggie grumbled. 'Spend the last five years trying to pay back a damn Yank for saving my life, and when I finally get even, he goes and finds himself a wife!'

Brett leaned back from Estelle. 'Means more work for you at the ranch.'

'Yeah?' Reggie snorted. 'Then it better mean more pay too!'

And the three of them laughed together. It sounded strangely out of place, echoing through the still mountain air — mirth and joy, after all the gunfire and death wails. But it seemed a good start to a happy ending.

THE END